One Drunk Text

Kathey Gray

Published in the United States of America
October 2018

Printed in the United States of America
November 2019

Cover Photo By: Belinda Strange

Cover Design: Made by Kathey Gray with Canva

Published by: Amazon KDP

One Drunk Text : a novel / by Kathey Gray

This book is dedicated to all my friends I've made over the years. I will forever cherish the memories we've made.

For my always and my never.

The madness of love is the greatest of heaven's blessings. —Plato

CHAPTER ONE
Third Grade

My cat Louise meowed at me as I stared at my four-eyed freckled face in the mirror in resentment. I sighed as I pushed down my frizzy brown hair.

"When's it going to happen, Louise? When am I going to wake up beautiful?"

"Meow," Louise responded.

I turned to her, her orange body was curled into a circle on my wooden vanity.

"Easy for you to say, you always wake up beautiful." I scratched her under her chin. She lifted up her body in an arch, and I ran my hand down her soft fur, all the way up to her tail. She purred and rubbed against me.

I sighed. "I have to go to school now."

"Meowwww-wowwwwww," she voiced her feline complaint adamantly.

I turned and grabbed my red backpack. "Yeah, well I'm not too thrilled about it either. See 'ya later," I called to her, closing my door.

In the kitchen, my mom was wearing her apron. "I made pancakes, sweetheart," she said brightly.

I ran through our yellow kitchen in a hurry. I grabbed a pancake off of the plate and stuffed it into my mouth in my haste. "Phanks mom."

My mom seemed annoyed by my eating habits as she huffed, "have a good day, dear!"

I ran down the driveway to greet the bus. I loved living in Georgia. I loved the way the trees fell in mossy green curtains everywhere I went. The big yellow bus honked and I ran to it, climbing on. I made my way to the back of the bus towards my best friend, Roberta.

She waved at me and jumped up and down in her seat. "Have you heard the new scoop?" She grinned from ear to ear as I sat beside her.

I adjusted my red backpack. "No, what?"

"We're getting a new student, a *boy*," she waggled her eyebrows at me.

Roberta was, in my opinion, the prettiest girl in our grade. With her wide crystal blue eyes, fair skin and dark brown hair, her beauty was obvious. But everyone else seemed to think Michelle Steinbeck was prettier, just because she had blonde hair and her family had more money.

I took another bite of my pancake. "Spho?"

She looked disappointed. "What do you mean *so?* What if he's cute? Don't you *care?*"

I chewed the on dry pancake, shrugging. "Doesn't matter, he'd never go for me anyway. And besides, who needs a stupid boyfriend?" I looked out of the window, watching the way the trees blurred together in a sheet of green.

Roberta was quiet for a moment, in contemplation. I thought she was going to drop it, but then she said, "I bet he's cute."

I rolled my eyes.

* * *

The school day continued on as usual, except for one thing. Roberta was right. The whole school seemed to buzz with tangible excitement at the acknowledgement of a new kid being on campus. I hadn't seen him yet, and I didn't really care to. I was walking outside to my next class when I heard a familiar obnoxious voice. It was the voice I hated even more than Mrs. Fillmore's, my most evil Math teacher. It was the voice of Billy Hughes.

I don't know the exact time Billy Hughes decided to be my bully, all I knew was that it had gone on for longer than I wanted to admit. My mom told me it was because he had a crush on me. I found that to be very unlikely. Not only did it not make sense, but I didn't know of *one* boy in the *whole* school that had a crush on me. My mother also told me that I was the prettiest girl in Savannah, Georgia, mind you. You can see where I developed my skepticism.

Anyway, this day wasn't different from any other. New kid or not, every day Billy would find a way to bully me. It was just the natural order of things.

"Hey Corinne, I thought they didn't let *dogs* in the school!" he yelled behind me.

I quickened my pace, ignoring him.

"Don't you think it's *weird*, Landry?" he said to his equally mouth-breathing friend.

"*Yeah!* She probably has *fleas!*" Landry agreed, shouting.

I began to run and I heard them come up close behind me, their footsteps pounding the dirt. I felt one of them grab my backpack, jerking me back.

"Let go!" I protested.

I was swung around and I almost fell on the ground. Once I was turned facing them, Billy let go. "You know the drill, four eyes. Lunch money?" He towered over me, holding out his chubby palm expectantly.

He really was *ugly*. If it hadn't been for his size, I thought he might've been on the opposite spectrum of the bullying field. He had dishwater blonde hair and beady eyes. His lips seemed to be perpetually curled into a sneer, exposing his gnarly, cavity-filled mouth full of silver teeth.

I don't know what set me off this time, but I surprised myself by spitting out the word, "*no*."

My eyes widened at the same time as his. I was surprised by my own boldness.

Landry, his red-headed friend, laughed beside him. Billy didn't like that very much. He turned red in the face and sweat beaded on his forehead. He grabbed me by the straps of my backpack.

"*What* did you just say, Alpo Girl?" he challenged, pressing his sweaty forehead against mine and forcing me to stare him in his evil, beady eyes. *Geez, his breath reeked.*

My heart hammered in my chest and sweat began to cool the back of my neck. "I mean...*yes?*" I questioned.

Billy released me with a smug grin. "That's what I thought." Then he held out his hand again.

I sighed and dug my hand into my pocket, the crumbling bills sticking to my sweaty palm. My cheeks burned hot and red, I was humiliated.

Billy snatched the money from me. "Don't *ever* talk to me like that again," he warned, before shoving me back with both of his hands.

I fell flat on my butt with a '*humph*' in the damp grass. Tears formed in my eyes and I quickly wiped them away.

"You might want to check that money for fleas, Billy," Landry teased.

They both started barking at me. I stared at the ground, silently wishing it would swallow me up. They started to turn to walk away, when I heard the sound of flesh smacking against flesh. My head shot up just in time to see Billy's head turn almost all the way around. My jaw fell open as he, like a demolished building, fell with a heavy thump to the ground, cloud of dust and all. Landry was next, I saw the boy punch him straight in the jaw. He fell on the ground next to Billy, like two matching sacks of potatoes.

I slowly raised my eyes from the boys on the ground, to the boy who came to my rescue. The sun shone behind him, basking him in a heavenly glow, making him seem other-worldly. He was tall and muscular with dirty blonde hair and friendly, slanted, green eyes. Most of all, he was cute. Maybe he was a fifth grader?

He held out his hand to me, smiling. "Hi, I'm Garrett, the new kid."

CHAPTER TWO

21st Birthday

"What about this one?" Roberta came out of the dressing room in a short Emerald green dress with a low dip in the front, showcasing her impressive cleavage.

Roberta was still the most gorgeous girl I'd ever known. Which only intensified over the years. She had knocked Michelle Steinbeck out of the water by the 5th grade and had practically every boy lined up wishing to date her ever since.

My eyes widened and I tried not to stare. "Well the girls look great in it, so it's bound to draw attention to the opposite sex," I admitted.

She snickered. "You mean *men?*"

"Yes, men."

"You're such a prude, Corinne," she teased.

I rolled my eyes, adding, "plus I really like the color and the... sparkles," I gestured around my own neck, as if she couldn't locate the sparkles on her dress.

She grinned and checked herself out in the mirror. "I like it, too. I think I'm going to buy it."

I nodded.

"What about you, are you getting that black one?" She turned to me.

"Yeah," I nodded, absentmindedly, clutching the short dress in my hands.

My phone buzzed and I swiped the screen to read the message. My face fell instantly.

"What is it, what's wrong?" Roberta noticed immediately. She was so intuitive when it came to my emotions. I guess being friends for fourteen years could do that.

"Nothing," I shrugged, trying to pull my lips back upward from the frown they'd automatically set into.

She put her hands on her hips. "He can't come, can he?"

I shook my head. "He has to work," I explained.

She scoffed. "I've heard that one before, he's probably just got another hot young thing he wants to roll around with in the sack."

I felt my insides crush. She was probably right.

"I mean who needs him anyway, right? I sure the hell don't want him around scaring off all the potential guys I could be meeting tonight," Roberta quipped.

Right again. Whenever he was around, other men seemed too intimidated to approach us. Not that *I* minded much. I nodded again.

"Look, I know he's your other 'best friend' or whatever," she rolled her eyes and held up her fingers, sarcastically making air quotations. "But we don't need *Garrett Simmons* to have fun," she raised a brow at me.

I stood up. "You're right."

As we paid for the dresses, I tried to remind myself of just that.

* * *

We met up with more friends of mine and Roberta's from the shop. We ran a small boutique together that sold coffee, books, candles, t-shirts and cards, called 'Vintage Only'. We had only been open for a year and a half, and the business had taken off in way that no one could anticipate.

We had dinner at a cute champagne bar a block away from the store. I nibbled on all kinds of appetizers, but they didn't have much for actual *food*. I knew my diet would mostly consist of liquid tonight anyway. Afterwards, we went to the pub on the next street and ordered beers around the house. Everything was going well, but I could feel myself getting more and more drunk by the moment. First the champagne, then the beer. I went to the restroom after an hour, hoping I didn't look as messy as I felt.

I'd come a long way since grade school, and although I wasn't as attractive as Roberta, I didn't look like 'Alpo girl' anymore either. By junior high I had finally discovered the miracle of contact lenses and the magical instrument known as the 'flat iron'. By high school I'd developed enough curves to not be mistaken for a boy. I'd also learned how to do my makeup and had developed a 'socially acceptable' fashion sense. Being best friends with Roberta didn't hurt either. She'd actually began her modeling career in high school and was a big help for me in getting myself together.

I stared at my reflection. The black dress hugged my curves in all the right places. My cat-eye eyeliner had somehow fared well and my brown hair still slicked down my back, shiny and calm as ever. I slipped my lipstick out of my purse and applied more of the wine color to my lips. The color complemented my brown eyes and my pale, freckled complexion. I shrugged, satisfied and went back out.

"There you are, my lady! Look what I got us," Roberta waggled her eyebrows at me. "*Tequila*," she winked.

My eyes fell to the shots lined up on the bar counter. "Oh my, that you did," I muttered nervously.

"Time for shots!" She called, picking one up and handing it to me.

April and Rebecca from work both cheered and picked one up. "To my best friend's twenty first birthday!" she announced, clinking her glass against mine.

"To *me*," I laughed and sipped down the shot, blanching. "Ugh, *strong*," I complained.

Roberta giggled. "Well, it *is* Tequila, silly! Don't worry, we're going to Uber! You can have as much as you want!" She reassured me.

"*Great*," I widened my eyes.

Roberta chuckled. "This place is boring, let's go somewhere else," she rose suddenly, laying down a twenty.

I eyed the money and she smiled reassuringly. "It's your birthday, my treat."

"Okay," I conceded.

I don't remember much after that. Everything became a blur of shots, guys trying to get in my face, and a lot of dancing with Roberta. I know we went to at least three more bars and one club. But I *definitely* lost count of my drinks. I vaguely remembered the car ride home in the Uber, in which I passed out in several times. I sort of remember stumbling up the stairs to mine and Roberta's apartment, her and I, arm in arm, giggling as we went.

But I sure as *hell* don't remember texting anyone, which was my rude awakening.

The bright sun beamed onto my face, burning my skin. I turned my face away, back onto my cool, inviting pillowcase.

"Wake up sleepyhead, I made coffee," I heard Roberta call.

Why is she already up? Morning people! Well, I'm a creature of the night. A vampire. Allergic to sunlight before 10 a.m.

"No," I grumbled.

"Come on, don't you want to look at these pictures from last night? They're fucking hilarious," she snickered.

Pictures? Shit. More like *evidence!*

"No thanks," I mumbled into the pillow.

She walked over and set down a steaming mug of coffee beside me on the nightstand. "Here, *drink*," she commanded. "We have work to do at the shop, inventory," she informed me, before turning to walk away. "I'm going to take a shower, you should probably get up."

I groaned in complaint. Roberta could party like no other, but she also could *work* like no other.

I sat up, slipping on my glasses, and took a sip of the coffee, closing my eyes at the instant effect it had on my body. It warmed me inside and brought my bones back to life.

"Mmm, yes," I mumbled to myself.

I opened my eyes again to check my phone. The time read 9:15 a.m. My messages were brought up on the screen and I furrowed my eyebrows. *Who was I messaging? I don't remember messaging anyone last night.* I opened the strand and my mouth fell open. My eyes bugged out of my head. A cold sweat instantly broke out all over my body, and my heart raced dangerously fast. I felt sick. *Oh,* I was going to be sick. I smacked my palm over my mouth and ran as fast as I could to the kitchen trash can, where I emptied the contents of last night's liquid diet into it, heaving over and over again. As soon as I was done, I stumbled back to my phone, re-reading the message repeatedly.

What. The. Hell!!!! No!!! What the *hell?* I didn't write that, *did I?* I would *never* write that! I would never be *that* stupid! Even as drunk as I had been! *Right....?*

I stared at the message, not having one clue of what to do.

Garrett

3:23 a.m.   Garrett Simmons, I'm in love with you.

15

CHAPTER THREE
Fourth Grade

"Race you to the monkey bars, Corinne." Garrett's eyes gleamed, a teasing smile lighting his face. He started jogging in place in anticipation of my answer.

"No," I whined.

"Why?" He stopped jogging and stood in disappointment.

"Because you always *win*," I complained.

He bit his lip. "*Please*, c'mon I'll let you win this time." He stepped closer to me, lining up his body next to mine.

I grew quiet, deliberating.

He stepped backward four times and my eyes followed the motion. "I'll start from here and I'll let you have a 30 second head start," he encouraged.

"Fine," I pouted.

A wide grin spread across his face. "Ready, set, *go!!!*" he shouted.

I took off as I heard him counting backwards from thirty. I was halfway to the monkey bars, when I heard him say one. I pushed my legs as hard as I could. The hard ground jolted up them and into my hips, rattling my bones. I could hear Garrett's strong but steady footfalls right behind me. He was gaining on me and fast. He ran beside me before we could both reach out. My hand met the metal bars a millisecond before his did. I jumped up and down in elation, squealing. When I finally stopped to stare at Garrett, he smiled warmly at me.

"See, you don't always lose, Corinne. You beat me, fair and square."

I knew he let me win, and he'd also given me the head start, but I didn't say anything. He was as fast a gazelle and was on the football and soccer teams. It was those small moments that made me start to fall for Garrett Simmons. Times when he *could've* been mean, he could've gloated, he could've proved me wrong, and he just *didn't*. Anyone else would've rubbed it in my face. That's how I knew he had a heart of gold.

I still never understood why he decided to be my friend. At first I thought he did it because he felt sorry for me. But after a few months, I realized he had become as close to me as Roberta. Garrett's family was from Wisconsin and had moved here so his dad could open a factory of his own to run in Savannah. Meaning his family was much more well off than mine. They had a two story house with land and our house was small and in a residential area. It made the fact that he was my friend even *more* confusing. We did have a lot in common though. We both liked to climb trees, read, ride bikes and hang out in the clubhouse with Roberta. We also both loved our pets, except he had a dog named Henry and I, a cat named Louise.

Roberta had accepted him into our little trio warmly enough, and it was nice to have a boy around to chase off bullies or fix things whenever we needed. But Garrett had *lots* of friends, not just Roberta and I. He was friends with almost everyone. But no matter how much I thought he'd forget about us and move on, he never did.

We were inseparable from sunrise to sunset.

One day, when we were in the girls bathroom at school, I decided to ask Roberta a very important question.

"Roberta, do you think Garrett is cute?"

She stared at herself in the mirror, brushing her hair with a small purple brush. "Duh, of course, he's a total *babe*," she turned to me and winked.

I smiled crookedly and wiped it off. "But... do you *like* him?"

She cut her eyes to me, shrugging. "He's my best friend, Corinne, that'd be *weird*. He's like my brother now, you know?" She explained.

I nodded. "Yeah."

She paused and the bathroom grew silent. She turned to me. "Why, do *you* like him?" I heard interest rise in her voice.

My eyes fell to the floor. "*No!* No, I feel the same as you. He's like my brother," I shrugged awkwardly.

She nodded, dropping it.

But deep down, I felt it. The lie. I didn't feel that way about him at all. But was I ever going to admit that to Roberta or anyone else? Not 'till my dying day.

I'd never admit that his eyes made my heart flutter and his smile made my knees weak. That his voice calling my name was like the sweetest music I'd *ever* heard and that I'd *never*, in a million years, grow tired of it. That I'd race him to the monkey bars and lose every single day if it meant we could spend recess together. And that every day I saw him walking in the hall, I had to remind myself of how to breathe properly. Or that every time he grabbed my hand, my heart would stop beating for just about three seconds.

But I kept it a secret because I knew, deep down, there was no way on *Earth* he could possibly feel the same way about me. It just wasn't worth the risk of losing him as best friend. It was a secret I'd never even admit to *Roberta*. I was too afraid that one day she'd accidentally blurt it out to *Garrett*. I was too happy with our little circle of friends. If I could keep it a secret that Roberta had gotten kissed by Danny Braverman under a Georgia Moss tree after we went to the carnival last summer, then I could certainly keep *this* a secret.

It was just my heart after all. I imagined it like one of those diaries that had the heart lock and key. I'd keep my secret safe inside, locking it up and hiding the key. Maybe one day I'd tell him, when I was ready. I just wasn't ready yet.

Fourth grade was another great year for all of us and when summer came, we spent our days and nights always together. We'd hang out in the clubhouse, we'd go swimming in the lakes and at the local pools. We rode our bikes everywhere, to the library, to get ice cream, to each other's houses, you name it.

But when the fifth grade came, so did a girl sent from Hell itself. Summer Whaley arrived, just in time to ruin my life.

CHAPTER FOUR
Truth Serum

Delete

Oh fuck. Oh fuck, what did I just *do?* What did I just *do?!?* I drunk texted Garrett, my best friend and secret love for the last twelve years that I'm in *love* with him?!? Why would I *do* that?!? Oh, that's right, because I was wasted off my *ass!*

Shit. Fuck. Dammit. Shit-fuck. Mother-fucking shit!

And now I just *deleted* it! Wait... had he *read* it yet? Why the fuck didn't I check to see if he'd *read* it?!? Oh my God, *did he read it?* I started to hyperventilate when Roberta walked in, wearing only a towel.

"Hey, what's wrong?" She rushed over to me. "Are you okay?" She crouched down and stared me in the eyes. "Why does it smell like *vomit* in here?" She held her nose.

"I threw up in the trash can," I answered robotically, my shaking hand still holding my phone.

"O-kay. Is that why you're breathing like that?" She eyed me, worried.

I shook my head slowly from side to side in a daze. She sat down beside me. Her hair was wrapped up in a towel and I stared at it blankly. "Tell me what's going on, you look upset." She gently put her hand on my knee.

I took a deep, shaky breath. I had no other choice now but to come clean. "I drunk texted Garrett."

She seemed confused. "So?"

I turned slowly to look at her. "I told him I was *in love* with him!" I said, emphatically.

Once again she looked confused. "So, just tell him you're sorry, and that you didn't mean to mess with him— that you were drunk." She shrugged it off.

I continued to stare at her.

She gasped. "Unless it's *true?*"

My eyes fell to the wooden floor and I began to hyperventilate again. Her eyes widened and even she started to panic. She'd never seen me act like this. "Okay, it's okay." She looked around. "Just, just calm down. I'm going to go get you some water. Just...stay right there and don't pass out!" She rushed off holding her towel up.

I fell flat on my back staring at ceiling, the stale taste of vomit and alcohol lie stagnant on my dry tongue.

Water wasn't going to fix this. I needed to know if he'd read that text. But I also *didn't* want to know if he had, because if he *did...*

Nope. I couldn't even think about it.

"Here, sit up. Drink this," Roberta commanded.

I rolled over and sat up, taking the glass from her. I gulped and gulped until the water was gone. Then I set it back down on the nightstand.

Roberta was careful when she asked. "Now tell me *exactly* what you said," she prompted.

I put my head in my hands, resting my elbows on my knees. "I said, 'Garrett Simmons, I'm in love with you'," I murmured into my palms.

I heard a sharp intake of breath beside me. "Those *exact* words?" She questioned.

"*Yes*," I groaned, refusing to look at her.

"Shit. You really don't beat around the bush," she mumbled.

My head shot up and I glared at her. "It was an *accident*, Roberta!!" I insisted.

"Alright, alright. I know. I'm sorry." She held up her hands.

I sighed and my head fell back into my hands. There was a pause of silence.

"Wait—maybe, maybe he didn't *read* it yet!" She bounced on the bed, holding out her hand. "Let me see." She reached for my phone.

I looked up at her. "It's too late, I deleted it before I could check," I exhaled in exhaustion.

"Why would you *do* that?" She accused.

"I panicked!" I admitted shamefully.

We both sat there quiet again.

"Well, nothing you can do now but wait for him to reach out to you." She put her hands on her hips.

"Yeah," I shrugged.

"Do you really, though?" She turned to me with a curious look on her face.

"Yes," I sighed. "I love him, I'm in love with him, and I have been since the third grade."

Her eyes widened and her mouth fell open. "Wow. You really hide things *well*," she smiled, impressed.

"I *did*," I grimaced.

"It'll be alright. Let's go in to work to get your mind off of things," she encouraged, reaching out to rest her palm on my shoulder.

I nodded in agreement and she stood up and walked towards her room to get dressed. When she was almost to her room she called, "and take out that fucking trash, it stinks!"

I reluctantly did as she asked, then dragged myself into the shower. I couldn't stop thinking about the daunting words and worrying that he *did* read the text. What an *idiot* I am! Why *Garrett?* Why did I have to pick *him* out of *everyone* in my contacts?!? But deep down I knew. Something about being under the influence, it always brought your most secret desires to the surface. Fucking truth serum.

What will he *think* of me? I fucking blew it. Everything... all of our years of friendship and trust, all gone and out the window. It felt crushing. Suddenly the shower was too hot, too steamy, and too claustrophobic. I felt like I was going to faint. I had to get out. I turned off the water and stepped out, wrapping myself in a towel. I walked over to the steamy mirror and wiped away the condensation. I stared at my reflection, but instead of seeing the woman I'd become, I just saw that nerdy little girl again.

Garrett Simmons would never want me. He had grown into a dreamboat of a man, dating models and even some of the lesser known actresses. I always knew he would though, just like I'd always known I wouldn't be enough for him. But like they say, you take what you can get. And I was willing to spend forever holding back, just to be able to have him in my life as a friend.

But now, everything was going to change. I was going to lose him.

* * *

I kept checking my phone at work, wondering when he'd message me and what he'd say. I was horrified that he might actually *call* and I'd have to talk to him in *person* and die of humiliation live. I was even more horrified that he might *never* message me, *ever* again. That he'd ghost me completely. That would hurt even worse.

But at exactly 1:30 p.m. my phone buzzed. Roberta and I were in the cafe section of our store, restocking our coffee and cream. We both turned to look at each other at the same time.

"Corinne, *don't—*" She warned with her eyes.

We both ran to my phone on the counter at the same time. I picked it up first. The screen displayed a green message symbol with Garrett's contact name. But the message itself wasn't visible. "*Fuck!*" I breathed.

Roberta struggled with me, trying to pry the phone from my fingers. "Don't *look!* Let *me!*" She pleaded, afraid to see her friend get crushed.

"*No!* I can *take* it!" I fought back.

I yanked it back from her, but I stumbled over a rug and the phone went flying. Roberta and I watched in helpless desperation as it landed in the tall pitcher of our special recipe of whipping cream that was standing upright in the sink.

We both ran over to it and I reached in to pull it out. I pressed the side buttons of the phone in a frenzy, but it only lit up once, before dying completely, the screen going black.

My horrified face turned to Roberta's. "What *now?*" I whispered.

CHAPTER FIVE
Fifth Grade

Summer fucking Whaley breezed in with her long, golden hair and deep blue eyes and suddenly Garrett was awestruck. He asked to be her boyfriend almost immediately and like any sane eleven year old would, she said yes. Suddenly, he started spending every recess with her, not to mention she also annoyingly began to sit at our lunch table with us. It was *torture.*

The worst part was, I had to pretend to like her. And every time she opened her stupid, pretty mouth to speak, I daydreamed about punching her in the jaw. The second worst part was that I had to act unfazed by Garrett and her being an item. Roberta wasn't that fond of Summer either, but I knew for a fact that she didn't carry half the disdain that I had for her. She couldn't possibly, and she also didn't know that *I* did. It was hard for a while, and I'd started to wish that I didn't *feel* the way I did about Garrett. I'd even grown mean and resentful. One day when Summer was absent, Garrett asked me, "hey Corinne, you want to race?"

Yes, *yes. I want to race you and I want things to go back to the way they were before the blonde-haired devil showed up and stole you away from me*, I wanted to say. But of course I couldn't say that.

Instead, I made up a lame excuse. "I'm kind of tired, Garrett."

His face fell. "Oh, well okay, maybe next time."

I nodded and walked away. I wasn't sure why I did that, I guess I was protecting myself from him.

Another day, Summer was sick on a Friday leaving Garrett open for the weekend. "Hey, Corinne," he caught me on the bus. "You want to ride our bikes to get ice cream this weekend?" he asked.

I just want to kiss you, I thought. But of course I didn't *say* that, I could *never*.

"I can't. I have plans with my parents." I twisted my hair around my finger.

"Oh...that's ok," he answered, before walking back to his seat with his shoulders slumped.

I think he knew I was avoiding him, but he didn't know *why*. At least I hoped he didn't. I had to protect myself and avoiding him was the only way I knew how to do that. But I was *miserable*. I walked around with a constant ache in my chest and a lump in my throat.

My mom noticed and asked me about it. "Honey, have things been okay at school?"

I was sitting on our floral living room sofa watching TV. I turned around. "Yes, why?" I scoffed.

"Because you've been moping around for a while now. Is everything *okay?* You're not being bullied again, are you?" She walked around the sofa to come to sit by me. My eyes followed her until she sat down next to me, feeling the sofa slightly sinking down from her weight as she did.

"No, mom," I shook my head, turning away.

"Where has Garrett been? He hasn't been around in a while," she inquired.

I felt my body stiffen at the sound of his name and had to fight from flinching. *His* name always did that to me.

I turned back to her, studying her womanly features. She was much prettier than me with soft brown curls, fair skin and blue eyes. Maybe if I'd gotten my looks from *her* I wouldn't be in this boat. Maybe I *would* be 'Summer' and I'd already be dating Garrett. But no, I had to look like my dad, with frizzy brown hair, plain brown eyes and freckles. *What a curse!*

"I don't know, mom. I guess he's been busy. Playing sports, or whatever it is that boys do," I shrugged.

She furrowed her delicate brow. "Still, he always makes time to come play with you."

Her words stung even though I already knew all too well that I'd been side-lined by Garrett. I blinked hard at the tears that were trying to ruin my secret and stared at the TV in an attempt to hide my eyes.

"It's *nothing*, mom. Besides we're getting kind of old to 'play' anyway. We're growing up," I straightened my shoulders, hoping to look convincing.

She sighed. "I suppose so. You're sure nothing's wrong?" She asked.

I turned to her and forced a smile. "No, mom, everything's fine." I lied through my teeth.

"O—kay. Oh and Roberta called, she said that she has some 'very important' news to tell you." She tilted her head towards the phone on the wall.

My attention was grabbed, and I shot up to call her back. "Thanks, mom."

I dialed Roberta's number, and she picked up on the first ring. "About *time!*" She complained.

"Sorry, I was talking to my mom. What's up? What's the important news?" I twirled the beige phone cord around my finger.

"Garrett broke up with Summer and he wants to hang out."

Elation ran through me and I had to hold in the scream of delight that threatened to explode from me. I twirled the cord even tighter around my finger until the blood circulation was almost cut off. "*Why?* Why'd they break up?"

"He caught her kissing Peter Allen at the pool."

"*Tramp!*" I muttered. But fear shot through me at my admission. I quickly turned to check and see if my mom had heard me, but fortunately her head was currently stuck in the refrigerator.

"Right," Roberta agreed. "So you want to ride bikes with us?"

"Yes, meet you at our clubhouse?" Excitement bubbled through me like a shaken up soda pop can.

"Sure! See you there!"

I hung up with Roberta and ran to get my tennis shoes on. As I shoved them on, my mom asked where I was going. I yelled to her my answer.

She smiled at me from over the counter as I opened the door to leave. "I thought you guys were getting too 'old' to play?" She teased.

"I guess not today!" I grinned back, before opening the door, shutting it swiftly behind me.

CHAPTER SIX
Breakfast Date

We both stared at the dripping phone like idiots. Finally I sighed and grabbed a towel, wrapping the phone in it and cleaning it off.

Roberta sighed too. "Fuck, Corinne. I am *so* sorry. I'll pay for a new phone for you."

I stared at the black screen, hopelessly. "It's okay, Roberta," I mumbled. "You know that's not why I'm *really* upset. I just...I'm afraid of what he's going to have to say, you know." I looked up to meet her crystal blue eyes. Her face was scrunched in discomfort.

"I know. Come here," she pulled me in for a hug. "It's going to be okay, I promise. Garrett *loves* you. The kind of love that can't just be erased overnight. You've spent years together. You've built a relationship, essentially."

Her cool silky hair brushed against my cheek. Her familiar perfume connected with the comfort center in my brain. "Yes, it's called a *friendship*," I muttered. "He's never seen me as anything more than a friend," I argued.

Roberta huffed and let go of me, exasperated. She grabbed me by the shoulders and shook me. Her blue eyes were fierce. "You don't *know* how he sees you! You're not *him!* For all you know, he could've been pining for you all this time, too! He could've been just as afraid as *you* were to say something!"

I flushed. "Whatever, Roberta. Like he'd ever even have time to think of me in between bagging model after model. His calendar is more booked with models than fashion week."

Roberta ignored me, prancing away on her tip toes. She held her hand over her heart and lowered her voice to a horrible impression of Garrett's. "Oh, Corinne! Where for art thou, Corinne? *When* will she notice that I'm secretly in *love* with her? When will she *cease* this torture? When will the suffering *end?* If she doth love me, I will surely *die!*" She twirled around and around in the empty cafe, and I couldn't help but snicker.

"Okay, okay. *Stop* Roberta. You're attracting a crowd," I laughed.

Roberta paused and turned around. Outside of our glass doors people were starting to gather and stare, perplexed by her behavior.

"Oh my God," she laughed, covering her mouth. She waved to them. "Our coffee here is *great* by the way!" She yelled, by way of explanation, skipping back to me. The onlookers carried on, wearing confused expressions.

"Hey, if this whole entrepreneur thing doesn't work out for us, I would say you might have future in show-business," I teased, nudging her with my elbow.

She giggled. "Shut up. Come on, let's clean this up so we can get out of here." She set back to action.

We cleaned up our mess and prepared lock up the shop. We were about to walk out the door, when Roberta's phone rang. She pulled the phone out of her pocket and her eyes widened.

"*What?* What is it?" I asked, panicked.

"It's *Garrett*," she whispered.

My stomach sank and my throat dried up. "So, answer it," I croaked. "He probably just wants to talk to *you* anyway," I squeaked.

She nodded once, licking her lips in concentration. A determined look filled her eyes. She swiped her finger across the screen then held the phone up to her ear. "Hello?"

"Hi...yes, she is." Her eyes met mine and mine grew even larger.

My stomach felt like a hollow pit. I was lightheaded and dizzy. Did he want to talk *now?* What would I *say* to him? I wasn't *ready!* Would I *ever* be ready?

"Oh, well she's been having phone trouble." Roberta's eyes landed on the black screen of the phone in my hand.

"Sure. Okay, tomorrow morning? Ten a.m.? Okay. Yes, I'll tell her," she nodded.

I shook my head vehemently. What was she *doing?* Making plans for me without *asking* me? With *Garrett?!?*

A giant smile lit up her face. I, however, had the expression of a serial killer.

"Okay, Garrett, talk to you later," she winked at me. She pressed end on the call and jumped up and down squealing. "He wants to have breakfast with you tomorrow!"

I felt like throwing up again. I felt the nausea bubbling up in my throat. I ran to the sink and dry heaved into the sink. A few minutes later, Roberta stood next to me with her hands on her hips.

"So dramatic," she shook her head.

I turned on the faucet and splashed cool water onto my face and made a cup with my hands, sipping water from it.

"Is this going to become a thing? Because there's this brilliant thing called toilets, you know," she complained.

I dried my face with a towel and stared daggers at her. "You. *Traitor*," I accused with fire in my eyes.

"You're *welcome!*" She said in a baby voice, reaching down to pinch my cheeks.

I swatted her hands away.

She began to walk out of the shop and I followed after her, stomping and silently brooding. We locked it up and walked to our car, getting in. Once we were seated, she turned to me.

"I did you a favor. You know what this *means*, right?"

"Tonight is my last night alive?"

She twisted her lips and shot me a look. "It means he wants into your panties, Corinne," she smiled wickedly.

My jaw dropped.

"Exactly what I thought. You know what *else* it means?" She raised her brows suggestively.

When I didn't answer, she continued. "It means he likes you *back*."

She put the car in drive and pulled out of the parking space swiftly. My back hit the seat, but I couldn't feel a thing. What if he *did* like me back? What if he *did* want in my panties? I thought about the way Garrett's body looked in swim trunks and gulped dryly. Suddenly *those* thoughts were even scarier than if he didn't feel the same way about me at all. I'd never even thought of these things as being a *possibility*.

Roberta looked over at me and chuckled. "Aw, poor thing is scared to death. Well, you'll feel better after we go shopping," she shrugged.

I turned to her, numbly. "Shopping?"

She nodded. "For an outfit that will make *everyone* want to get in your panties. And... probably some new panties, too," she winked.

My cheeks burned and she turned up the music, drowning out any objections I may have had planned.

I couldn't think of anything else to say, no intelligent words would form. I hoped to God I would be more capable of speaking tomorrow.

"Fuck me," I breathed.

CHAPTER SEVEN
Sixth Grade

I dabbed on the pasty concealer furiously. But no matter how much I put on, it still didn't cover the pea-size lumps on my face. *Stupid puberty.* Roberta laid on my bed, reading a 'Teen Beat' magazine. She didn't even look up from the pages as she spoke to me.

"You look fine, Corinne," she mumbled. "Whatever you put on is just going to wash off in the pool anyway, so it's kind of pointless."

I scowled in her direction. Roberta's skin was of course, flawless. She didn't have to wear makeup like I did. It just wasn't fair how some girls had all the luck. I ignored her and moved onto the next step. I picked up the mascara and unscrewed the lid, dousing the wand in the black liquid. Right before I swiped it onto my lashes, I turned around.

"You're sure this is waterproof, right?"

"*Yes*," she groaned. "Are you almost *done?* If we don't hurry up all the high-schoolers will be there and they'll take over like usual," she complained.

"Yes!" I hissed. "I'm almost done!" I applied two coats to my lashes, then put my glasses back on.

Did she *not* understand how *hard* I was trying to look cute for Garrett? *Oh right, she didn't.* Because I still hadn't *told* her how I felt about him.

She dropped the magazine onto her face hopelessly and sighed deeply. "Garrett will be here any minute," she mumbled into the glossy pages.

Two seconds later, my doorbell rang.

"Corinne!" My mom called.

"I know! I'm coming!" I yelled back.

Roberta let the magazine slide to the floor and sat up, grabbing her things. A smile had finally found its way back to her face. She made her way to my door and I followed behind with my pool bag, tugging at my one piece. I was at that awkward stage where I didn't quite have the same curves as Roberta, but boys had started to ogle me. I didn't like it. Except for Garrett, he never ogled me. *God, I wanted him to ogle me.* I was embarrassed of my body and refused to wear a two-piece. Roberta carried hers off flawlessly. I envied her confidence.

We walked out to my living room to find Garrett waiting for us wearing nothing but swim trunks and a smile.

"Hey Roberta. Hey Corinne. You ready?"

I blushed furiously and nodded.

"*Been* ready!" Roberta smiled. "Bye Mrs. P!" She waved to my mom, leading the way to the front door.

"Bye kids, have fun," my mom smiled at Roberta and Garrett.

Garrett followed Roberta and I followed him. My mom stopped me as I passed and shoved a ten dollar bill in my palm. "Don't forget to wear sunscreen, you know how you burn, Corinne," she whispered into my ear, pulling me in for a quick hug.

"Yeah, *okay* mom. Thanks," I mumbled quickly.

I followed Roberta and Garrett out the door and onto the driveway. The bright summer sun was almost blinding as we retrieved our bikes from the driveway. Roberta and I put our belongings in our bike baskets. Garrett only had a towel slung around his shoulders. We hopped on and rode through the streets, the hot sun burning our shoulders from above.

* * *

By the time we got to the pool, I was so sweaty. I couldn't wait to jump into the cool water. We parked our bikes, locking them up with our chain locks.

I looked over at Garrett. He wasn't even sweating. He turned back to me and I looked at my flip flops, embarrassed to be caught staring.

"What's on your face, Corinne?" Garrett asked.

I looked up. "What?" I asked, internally panicking.

"Your face," he pointed. "Your eyes, they're black," he continued.

"What do you mean?" My cheeks burned even hotter.

Roberta walked over. "It's just her mascara," she huffed.

Mortified, I scrubbed under my eyes with my fingers. Garrett stared, confused.

"You said it was *waterproof!*" I hissed at her, quietly.

"It's fine," she stared at my face. "You can't even tell anymore."

I nodded, still feeling like I had a second nose or a third eye. We walked to the line and showed our passes, entering the pool.

"*Oh no!*" Roberta moaned.

I was about to ask what was wrong, when I peered from behind her and found my answer. We were too late. The high-schoolers had arrived. Girls in bikinis with body parts I hadn't acquired yet, giggled herded together in groups. Muscular boys with deep, booming voices jumped in and splashed around loudly.

"Should we go?" I murmured.

Roberta was silent.

"No, we should *stay*," Garrett answered.

He led the way to the lounging chairs and sat in between two chairs full of teenage girls. They giggled at him, but he ignored them.

Roberta and I looked at each other. Finally, she shrugged and smiled, following suit. I sighed and followed her. We set down our things and applied sunscreen, then made our way to the water. We did our best to swim and have fun around all the obnoxious noise and body odor. After a while, we all decided to jump off of the diving board. Roberta was first, she dove in gracefully. Garrett was next and he did a crazy flip. I walked up and prepared to dive when two teenage boys behind me started to fight. One knocked the other one onto the board hard and it wobbled. I turned around, trying to steady myself.

"Cut it out!" I yelled at them.

Since they were too immersed in their heated, hormone-induced man-rage, they didn't hear me. Lifeguards began to jog over to us. One of the boys slammed the other one down again, and this time I lost my footing.

"Sto—" My voice was cut off when I slipped, falling backwards and hitting my head on the diving board.

The next thing I remember was Garrett's mouth on mine. I'd died and gone to heaven. That was the only explanation for why this would be happening. Suddenly, I didn't mind being dead. I could feel his sinewy, lean, muscled body hovering over mine. And he was wet. Why was he wet? Oh, who cared, Garrett Simmons was kissing me and it was divine. I could practically hear the heavenly chorus of angels singing.

"Corinne! Wake up! Wake up, Corinne!" Roberta's panicked voice invaded my fantasy.

Wait, why was *Roberta* here?

Suddenly, a painful burning erupted in my lungs. *I couldn't breathe!* My eyes shot open, just as I spit the water from my lungs, into Garrett's face. I stared at him through my now water-dotted glasses.

Garrett coughed, laughing and wiping the water away from his face. "Glad you've come back to Earth, Corinne."

Garrett's wet hair hung in his eyes. He'd... *saved* me? He wasn't *kissing* me, he was giving me mouth-to-mouth. But his mouth *had* been on mine. His lips on my lips. That counted, didn't it? There was something in his slanted eyes that made me blush. But before I could study it further, Roberta pushed him out of the way.

"Oh my God, I thought you *died!*" She squeezed me so hard, crushing my chest.

"I thought I did, too," I gasped for air.

Roberta released me and I finally noticed the crowd that had gathered around us. Practically everyone at the pool was there. Apparently, I'd fallen into the water after hitting my head on the diving board and Garrett had pulled me out. The lifeguards that had been preoccupied in stopping the fight during the incident, had also joined us and were thanking Garrett for his fast thinking and reactions. They offered him a job when he turned sixteen.

The next time Garrett's eyes met mine, the strange look I'd saw in them earlier, had vanished.

Once again, Garrett had blown my mind. Would there *ever* be a day when he didn't fascinate me?

"Your mascara's smeared to hell, by the way." Roberta mumbled next to me.

CHAPTER EIGHT
Sleepy Juice

I twirled in the baby blue and yellow ruffled sundress, loving the airy material. "Ok, yes I'm definitely getting this."

"Don't forget *these!*" Roberta ran over, carrying a shiny pair of baby blue stilettos.

"What the fuck are *those?*" I scoffed.

Roberta pouted, jutting out her bottom lip. "Your *shoes?*"

"*Stilettos?* You do know this is for *breakfast,* right?" I raised my eyebrows.

"Duh! You do know this for *Garrett*, right?" She countered. *Damn, she had a point.*

I thought about the last women I'd seen Garrett dating. Their long, tan legs unwelcomely graced my memory. My eyes involuntarily fell to the shoes in Roberta's outstretched hand, then slid back to her face. A smile stretched across her face.

"That's what I thought," she said.

* * *

Later at our apartment, I couldn't sleep a wink. I tossed and turned, rehearsing what I would say and how I would explain myself. I played out every scenario in my mind, even the ones in which I prepared for things to go bad. But no matter how long I prepared or obsessed, I still didn't feel ready for this cataclysmic event to take place. I felt strung out, like I'd been drinking coffee all night, but I hadn't had a cup.

After lying restlessly for over three hours, I turned to check the clock in frustration. The time read 2:45 a.m.

Fuck!

I was going to look like absolute hell tomorrow! No matter how pretty the dress, or how shiny the heels, I was screwed. I knew my eyes would be puffy and still have bags under them, no matter how much concealer I applied.

I huffed and climbed out of bed, throwing my legs off of the side angrily. I headed straight to the kitchen and opened the fridge. I crouched to the bottom shelf and reached for the bottle of whiskey, grabbing it by its cold neck. I closed the fridge quietly in search of a shot glass. Opening the top cupboard, I selected one.

'LAS VEGAS!' It read. It had tiny, pink plastic dice built into the bottom of the shot glass, and they clinked inside of it quietly. I grinned as I recalled mine and Roberta's last trip there. We'd went with our families (which was a terrible idea on our parents' part) the summer of our junior year and stayed at Circus Circus. I remembered how our parents had tried to shield our innocent eyes from the vulgar cards that littered the floor and failed miserably. As an apology to us (or possibly just a bribe to keep us quiet) they let us pick anything in the store. I picked the shot glass and while my parents weren't the most pleased, they acquiesced and had agreed.

I unscrewed the lid of the bottle and poured myself a shot. I sighed and threw it back, welcoming the burn in my throat. I hoped to *God* Roberta wouldn't catch me doing this, I'd never hear the end of it! Plus she had just had the awful task of cleaning up the mess from my last and very recent hangover. Henceforth why I was in this predicament to *begin* with! When I still didn't feel tired, I poured myself another shot.

"Hurry up and *work!*" I whispered to the bottle of whiskey.

It didn't answer me.

I refilled the glass two more times, before giving up and drinking it straight from the bottle. After a few more chugs, my legs effectively grew heavy and I swayed to the side.

"Now, *that's* more like it," I slurred to myself.

Louise walked in. "Roawww," she meowed.

"Louise!" I whispered. "Come here, weezy-weezy!"

She jumped on the counter and sauntered over next to the bottle of whiskey.

"Meowrrr," she half purred, half meowed.

I raised my hand and she arched her back into my palm. Funny how no one ever thought she'd live past ten years old. Yet here she was, fourteen, still alive and kicking. Fit as a fiddle even. I loved that cat so much. Luckily for me, the feeling was mutual for Roberta. If she wouldn't have tolerated Louise, that would have been a deal breaker when it came to the subject of me and Roberta sharing an apartment.

Louise sniffed at the opened lid of the bottle of whiskey.

"Oh! *No*, Louise! That stuff is icky, icky for kitty, kitties!" I scolded her.

I quickly screwed the lid back on the whiskey bottle, alarmed of how light it was when I lifted it to put it back into the fridge.

Hope Roberta doesn't notice at least until after tomorrow!

I rinsed the shot glass, too tipsy to effectively wash it without waking Roberta now, and replaced it in the cupboard. I scooped up Louise and she tried to protest, wriggling in my arms.

"*Meowrrr.*"

"Shhh-shhh, weezy-weezy," I coo-ed to her. "It's *sleepy* time."

I stumbled over to my bed and plopped myself in it, holding onto Louise. I fell asleep with her warm, furry body in my arms.

* * *

"Oh *fuck*... Corinne! Are you *kidding* me? It's nine fifteen. Get *up!*" Roberta's loud voice chided.

I shot up. "What?" Louise jumped from my lap.

"Oh geez, you smell of *booze!* Corinne...why were you *drinking* last night?"

I stared up at Roberta's blurry figure. Reaching over to my bedside table, I slipped on my glasses and found her looking much clearer. She was looking crisp in grey yoga pants and a white spaghetti strap tank top. Her hair was tame in a sleek, low ponytail. Looking at her suddenly made me feel messy.

Guess I'm busted. "I couldn't sleep," I explained lamely, scrubbing my eyes with my palms. "Can you just text Garrett for me 'never mind'?" I prepared to turn over and go back to sleep.

I felt a clean slap across my face. My eyes popped open from the sting. I paused for a moment, in shock, then met Roberta's eyes.

"....*OW!*" I yelled at her angrily, rubbing my cheek.

"*No!* You are NOT backing out on this one, Corinne! You've waited twelve *years* for this moment, pony up!" Roberta pointed in my face ferociously. "Now, *what* are you going to *do?*"

"Eat breakfast?"

"*No!* You're going to go get your man!"

I stared at her, confused. Garrett wasn't my man, *was he?*

"I *said*, what are you going to *do?*" She repeated.

Too afraid to object and have the hell smacked out of me again, I cooperated better this time. "Go... get my man?" I repeated with little conviction.

Roberta huffed. "I SAID, WHAT ARE YOU GOING TO *DO?*" She screamed, a huge grin lighting her face. Her cheeks were warm with exertion. *Oh, good, she wasn't going to kill me.*

I paused, before yelling back. "GO GET MY MAN!"

"*That's* the spirit! Now go get in the shower, you have about fifteen minutes tops to look like an absolute fucking goddess."

"*Shit!*" I jumped up and ran to the shower.

* * *

Somehow we pulled off a miracle. Thank God for hair mousse. It was a fast and easy way to make my wet curls look presentable. I had exchanged my glasses for contacts, and put on a few coats of mascara and a hot pink shade of lipstick. I was wearing 'the' dress and the shiny blue stilettos. Roberta stood next to me as we watched Garrett sipping coffee through the glass windows of the café. Seeing him waiting there for me, erased all of the false confidence I'd thought I'd had. No pep talk was going to prepare me for meeting with him. Tony fucking Robbins couldn't convince me that this was going to go well.

There was a reason Garrett dated models. He was a complete smoke-show. He'd grown into twice the man he was in his youth. The man probably had Viking blood in him or something. He was tall and all muscle. His hair was cut into a clean fade and he had that delicious scruff on his face. He took care of himself, that much was clear. And that was just his *looks*. His *personality* was the real kicker. He was sweet, warm, caring, funny and always protective of me and Roberta.

Garrett was the whole package.

What was I doing here again?

Roberta saw my face, and turned me to face her, squaring my shoulders. "Now, *what* are you going to do?" She asked me one last time.

"Go get my man," I whispered breathlessly.

CHAPTER NINE
Seventh Grade

I looked myself over in the mirror, satisfied. The teal and black ribboned dress that my mom had fought with me about was just the right fit for my style. She'd wanted me to get something more girly, perhaps with lace or anything pink. But I'd begun to find my own fashion sense and had put my foot down. She'd reluctantly agreed with the dress, knowing she wasn't going to convince me to wear anything else, and knowing it would take a lot more energy to take me shopping again, than it would to let me win.

I wore my hair down and crimped, with black eyeliner and black heels to match.

Roberta walked in. "I'm really digging your whole punk rock look," she smiled.

"Thank you," I curtsied, tugging at the polyester material.

Roberta's hair was in a more suitable chignon. She looked flawless as usual, in a silk purple gown with a jewel encrusted bodice and matching purple heels. She had glitter on her eyelids and shiny lip gloss on her lips.

"Ready to go, girls?" My mom asked.

Me and Roberta exchanged excited glances. "Ready as ever, Mrs. P," Roberta smiled.

* * *

Of course we didn't have dates, we weren't old enough to. And we didn't have a snazzy limo to pick us up like Summer Whaley did. We got into my mom's station wagon and were on our way. My stomach flipped uncontrollably at the thought of dancing with Garrett. I mean, there was no way in *hell* it would happen, but the thought alone sent my heart into a frenzy. Roberta was excited to dance with her crush, Steven Canton. We bounced in our seats until my mom pulled up to the jr. high and dropped us off. I could see the bright flashing lights through the dark windows of the school gym. I could hear the music pounding, the bass trembled the windows. We walked in and perused the crowd. The gym smelled like perfume, strong cologne, sweat and body odor, typical for a jr. high dance. I ignored the dirty looks Roberta and I got as I searched for the person I came here to see. Garrett was surrounded by a crowd of girls, all vying for his attention and a chance for the next dance. My excitement turned into nausea. I sighed and turned the other way.

"Hey— there's Garrett!" Roberta pointed. "Let's go say hi!" She tugged me back in his direction.

"I want to get punch." I pulled on my arm, away from him and towards the ever-comforting punch bowl of regret.

"What are you *talking* about? We can get that after!" Roberta scoffed, pulling me back. *Damn, she was strong, and insistent.*

I sighed and turned around, letting her pull me toward the small crowd of misery. The most popular girls surrounded Garrett, including Summer Whaley, who'd never fully gotten over him. She was annoying as shit. I faced their perfect little circle with dismay. I knew I stuck out by the way they eyed my fashion choices for the night. They stared at Roberta with even *more* hatred. They saw *her* as a threat and *me* as a menace. The girls who were giggling annoyingly and touching Garrett more than I liked, grew quiet when Roberta interrupted.

"Hey, Garrett!" She cut in.

Garrett's attention was effectively diverted as his eyes landed on us. "Hey, Roberta," he smiled. He stepped forward out of the huddle of girls. "Corinne."

My cheeks burned. "You two look *great*!" He enthused.

"You...look great," I mumbled awkwardly. And he did. He was wearing black slacks and shoes and a sage green button up that matched his eyes. His hair was gelled, it made him look older.

"Thanks," he blushed a little.

Just then a slow song came on. My mouth dried up and I felt sick. My eyes searched for Roberta, but Steven Canton had already found her and was leading her to the dance floor. I couldn't feel my legs anymore. I was frozen in place.

"Do you want to dance, Corinne?" Garrett asked.

I turned back to face him, he was blushing slightly. From behind him, I could see Summer Whaley giving me a 'burn in Hell bitch' look.

I heard myself say, "sure."

Garrett took my hand in his and led me to the dance floor. Butterflies filled my stomach as the disco lights danced overhead. The glowing lights floated around us like fairies. It was magical. We moved to the center of the dance floor. Roberta and

Steven swayed next to us. Roberta gave me a wink and a smile. Garrett's hot hands found my waist and I felt like my skin was singeing from under the fabric of where he touched. I, very carefully, wrapped my arms gently around his neck. We began to sway along with the music. I recognized the song now, it was Aerosmith's 'I Don't Want to Miss a Thing.' I could smell Garrett's cologne and it was playing with my brain and heartbeat in ways I couldn't understand.

"So are you having fun?" He asked, looking down at me.

I shrugged. "Sure, I guess. I just got here," I answered.

I felt so embarrassed, like he could hear my thoughts. Like he knew how I felt deep down. *Could* he see through me? I panicked inside.

"Well, I'm glad you came. It's always more fun when you do," he said.

I met his eyes and he corrected himself quickly. "I mean, when you and Roberta come..."

I nodded. It was awkwardly quiet. "Your dress is really, um... unique," he added, smiling awkwardly.

I laughed a little. "My mom isn't a fan," I admitted.

"Well, it suits you," he flushed again.

"Thanks." My cheeks were so hot.

Something happened then, and it made me dizzy. Garrett leaned down just a fraction closer to my face, he had a funny look in his slanted green eyes.

My heart had somehow left my chest and now resided in my ears. It almost looked like Garrett was going to try to *kiss* me. "*Garrett?*" I whispered.

"Huh?" He seemed just as confused as me as he stared at my mouth.

Time stopped and we floated, or at least it *felt* like we did. Garrett inched closer and I stared at his lips, too. I was waiting for him to kiss me. Garrett Simmons was about to kiss me. What did I *ever* do *right?*

Roberta grabbed my arm, breaking the trance. Garrett flinched back.

"Steven is *tongue-ing* Summer Whaley!" She bawled.

I turned to her, birds still swirling above my head. "*What?*"

She pointed to the dance floor, to the spot where Steven and Summer were sucking faces. "What the hell?" I muttered.

Roberta sobbed next to me. "Come with me to the bathroom, Corinne?" She begged.

The song ended. I looked to Garrett, apologetically. "It's fine, Corinne, go," he insisted.

His cheeks were still flushed from the strange moment we'd shared. He let go of me, and my hands reluctantly released him.

Roberta dragged me away from him. I turned and stared at him standing alone in the middle of the dance floor. I'd been thisclose to kissing Garrett Simmons.

I wasn't sure I'd ever get the same chance again.

CHAPTER TEN

Moment of Truth

As soon as I opened the door, the thick aroma of coffee hit me like a wall of awakening. It stunned me and I turned, ready to bolt.

I can't do this. I can't do this. What am I doing?

I caught a sight of Roberta through the glass window, and she waved at me, giving me a thumbs up. I smiled back, but I'm sure it looked more like a frown. She knew what I was about to try to do, which was to bail completely on my whole 'coming clean to Garrett' plan. I turn back around. The cafe is buzzing to life with people and their chatter. Some cute indie music is playing and the cool air surrounds me. Garrett is reading a newspaper and still hasn't noticed my arrival. I force my baby blue heels forward.

Right foot, left foot, and repeat. There, progress! I'm almost to the table, and Garrett looks up. When a man on his phone rushing by with his order in hand bumps into me, causing me to trip in my heels and go flying towards the table. I land directly onto Garrett, who catches me in his strong arms. I was already flushed and sweating everywhere now, as if I needed *more* reasons to be nervous.

"Woah— Corinne, are you alright?" He held onto me firmly.

Yes. Just hold me like that and...

"Hey— buddy, you need to *watch* where you're going!" He shouts at the man, who rudely continued on his route, without stopping to check on me or apologize. The man stopped at the door and waved him off before exiting.

"Prick," Garrett muttered under his breath.

Garrett helped me up and I righted myself, adjusting my dress.

"Thanks, and I'm okay. Guess that's what I get for wearing heels," my cheeks burned.

"Ha-ha, yes, I can understand that. I know they're not your usual style," he smiles.

I sit in the seat opposite of him, but not before I catch him checking out my legs. *What the hell?* Maybe this was going to go...*well?*

"Yeah, well, trying new things I suppose," I smiled shyly.

Garrett's eyes meet mine. "Nothing wrong with that." The twinkle in his eye makes a wave of astonishment run through me.

What the *fuck* is happening? Is Garrett actually *flirting* with me? Is Garrett fucking Simmons *actually* flirting with *me?!!*

I feel like every nerve in my body is buzzing with awareness and if he touches me, I might just jump out of my skin. The waitress walks over and takes my order. I order a cappuccino. She brings it back promptly and I carefully sip it. Outside, it's began to rain.

"So..." he starts.

My heart starts to beat slow and hard in my chest. "So..." I repeat, chewing on my lip and staring into my coffee.

"I think we need to talk about that text," I hear him say.

"*Do we?*" I cringe.

He chuckles and the sound is irresistible. I peek up at his eyes and back down again.

"Yes, we do," he says.

I look up at him, and his face is serious. His cheeks are heated. He *really* wants answers. *Oh, God.*

"Well, I do have to admit that I was stinking drunk when I texted you that," I laugh.

"I figured." His eyes crinkled at the corners. "Did you *mean* it?" He asked suddenly.

There was that serious look again. Garrett was sincere. This wasn't a joke to him at all.

I laughed again, I was *so* uncomfortable. "Um, I didn't *not* mean it..." My eyes found the table again.

"Corinne..." he whispered softly.

My face was burning and for some idiotic reason, tears began to form in my eyes. *Actual fucking tears!*

'My God! Don't you *cry*, you *idiot!'* I was yelling to myself in my head. *Who was in charge of my body right now?* Because I thought *I* was! And *I* would *never* let this happen!

But for some horrible reason, one tear escaped and slid down my cheek, landing in my cappuccino.

"Oh, Corinne," Garrett sounded crestfallen.

I laughed again, but it was pathetic. I wiped at my face. "I'm sorry, I'm fine. I don't know why...I don't know what's wrong with me," I shook my head, regretfully.

I looked up at him and he was staring at me with a look I've never seen before. Wait... I *had* seen it before. Only, it was a long time ago. I'd only seen glimpses of it though, this was the full on version. I sipped my coffee. I guess he got his answer.

The rain continued to pitter-patter outside of the window. I stared at it, admiring the way it landed in the puddles in big splashy drops.

"How *long?*" I heard Garrett whisper.

I shrugged, not wanting to meet his eyes. (Since the day I met you, oh, about twelve years ago to be exact.) "A while."

"Why didn't you *tell* me?" I felt his warm hand wrap around mine and I looked down at it. His hand was so large and warm enveloping my small, cold hand.

I shrugged again, then met his eyes. They were wide and earnest. "I didn't really think you'd feel the same," I admitted. "And you had a lot of other girls to stay busy with."

He sighed deeply and scrubbed his free hand against his mouth and cheek stubble.

"You're *wrong,*" he said in a low voice.

I blinked. *Does he mean?* My heart fluttered in my chest and felt like it expanded and then popped like a balloon filled with blood. It felt like the blood spilled and poured through my chest and to every limb of my body, warming them to life.

He looked down at our hands and traced soft circles onto the top of mine with his thumb. Tingles ran through me as I realized he'd never touched my hand like that before. Then he ran his thumb softly across my knuckles. Somehow he managed to make even *that* gesture intimate. "You're not the only one who's been holding back, Corinne," he said, his voice was husky now.

My heart began to race and I felt a little dizzy. "Oh."

Garrett dropped his hand from his mouth. "You want to get out of here?" He asked suddenly.

My frantic eyes met with his wild green ones. "And go where?"

"My apartment," he rasped.

"Oh, uh..."

Before I could decide, he withdrew his hand from mine and reached for his wallet. He laid the bills on the table and slid the wallet back in his pocket.

"Thanks," I said, in response to him paying for my coffee.

He nodded, taking my hand and pulling me to my feet. I felt like I was dreaming, as he held my hand and walked out of the cafe with me.

As soon as we were outside in the dewy sheets of rain, Garrett whirled around and grabbed my face in his hands. "Corinne," he whispered against my lips. The cold rain peppered down onto our heads and our bodies, drenching us. He steered me backward until my back was pressed against the brick wall of the cafe. Here under the awning, we got less rained on, but it still sprinkled our way.

He parted my lips with his tongue and all was lost.

CHAPTER ELEVEN
Eighth Grade

We were all having a slumber party at our mutual friend Nina's house. She'd invited me, Roberta, and our other friend Lindsay over. We'd started off the night right with pizza and chick flicks, but as the evening progressed, we'd moved on to more daring activities. We were all gathered in her upstairs bedroom.

"Okay, hold the ice cube until it's numb. I'm going to burn the needle," Nina instructed me.

I nodded. A moment later, she returned with the half of the apple and the needle in hand. She slid the apple behind my ear lobe, holding it in place, as she sat on the bed in front of me. "On the count of three, okay?" She said, with a determined smile on her face.

"Okay," I answered nervously. A smile was tugging at the corners of my lips for some unbeknownst reason.

Nina nodded. "One...two..." She held my gaze, lifting the needle. "*Three*."

I felt the needle pierce through my ear, but just barely. Nina pulled it back out and removed the apple, admiring her handiwork. She quickly replaced it with an earring, smiling. "Ready for the next one?"

After those of us who had bravely decided we needed our ears pierced for the first, or second time (I was the latter), were finished, we decided to look for more trouble and entertainment.

"I know what we should do! Friday Night Under The Street Light!" Nina exclaimed.

Roberta gasped. "Yesssssss!"

I giggled. "I'm down!"

So the four of us snuck down the dark staircase of Nina's house, stifling our giggles, and whisper-laughing. Everyone but us in the house was sleeping. Including Nina's little sister, Tatum, who would've totally ratted us out. We quietly opened the door and slipped out into the dark night. The corner streetlight glowed and beckoned us. We ran like a wild pack of hyenas into the night, screaming and stripping off our clothes. It fell to the ground in a scattered mess, until we were wearing our bras and panties only. We danced and cartwheeled, basked in the orange glow of the streetlight. We skipped and ran up and down the street, screaming like wild banshees. It was Roberta's piercing shriek, however, that halted my little outdoor striptease.

"*Oh my God*, it's *Garrett!*"

I froze in my tracks and turned around.

"And *Jackson!*" Lindsay yelled.

"Oh, *shit!*" Nina laughed.

How could we be so *stupid?* We knew Jackson lived across the street, but we didn't expect him to be outside at *two a.m.!* And since when did he hang out with *Garrett?*

Jackson let out a whistle. "*Yeah, baby!*"

My cheeks burned so hot. I didn't think I could be *more* embarrassed, until my eyes found Garrett. He was standing stock still next to Jackson, who was sitting in a chair on his porch. His mouth was hanging open a little and underneath his cap, he looked completely shocked.

We gathered our clothes in a frantic rush, covering our bodies while Jackson continued to goad. "Aw, Don't stop *now*, girls! It was just getting *good!*"

We ran back to Nina's front door screaming, but not before I could hear Jackson call us back once more.

"*Nina!*" He laughed. "Roberta, Corinne, *come back!*"

"*Lindsay!*" he begged. "Come *on!*"

We fought our way inside and stumbled up the stairs, much more loudly than necessary. We bursted into Nina's room, laughing hysterically. At least *they* were laughing. *I* was mortified. Garrett had seen me in my bra and panties *only!* We replaced our clothes and tried to settle down. Until the phone in Nina's room rang and we all screamed collectively.

Nina ran over to it. "*Hello?*" She answered breathlessly.

"It's *Jackson!*" Her hand flew to her mouth, covering her laugh.

Everyone huddled together on Nina's bed, giggling and whispering. I, however, felt the cold claw of death in the middle of my chest.

"*What?*" Nina laughed. "*No*, we're not coming out there again!"

She paused and then winked at us. "Why don't you and Garrett Simmons give us a strip tease?" She teased.

"That's what I thought. Wait, *what?*" She laughed.

Nina's eyes met mine as she giggled. "Is that *so?* He said *that?*" A huge grin lit her face. "About *Corinne?*"

Roberta and Lindsay gasped and turned to me. All eyes were on me and my face heated. "What did he *say?*" Roberta leaned forward, intrigued.

Nina ignored Roberta. "Why doesn't he want me to tell?" She continued to taunt Jackson further.

"*What* did he *say?*" Roberta repeated impatiently.

Nina argued with Jackson, before deciding against the boys' wishes. "Garrett said he's never seen Corinne dance like that," she chuckled, turning red.

The girls screamed and pushed at me, playfully.

"*Ooohhh*, Corinne," Roberta teased.

"He likes your body— in *motion*," Lindsay joined in, swaying her own hips in display.

I dropped my face into my hands, thoroughly humiliated. "Stop, guys," I muttered into my hands.

But I couldn't help the thrill that worked its way through me.

What the hell does that even *mean?* I wondered. He liked the way I looked while I danced half dressed? Or worse, he was disappointed by my reckless behavior? Did he think I was trashy or something? I didn't want him to look down on me.

"What's he saying *now?*" Roberta asked.

Nina held out the phone. "He hung up!" She hooted.

Everyone laughed, before we moved on to the next phase of the sleepover, the junk food phase. After we gorged on soda, brownies, chips and candy, we were feeling dangerous again. We played a game we'd seen on the movie *The Craft*, called "light as a feather, stiff as a board." We all screamed when we could swear that Roberta *floated*. It didn't work on me of course, which didn't surprise me. We told our scariest ghost stories and confessed our crushes. I, naturally, insisted that I didn't have one.

Then we all hunkered down in Nina's big bed and snuggled up, watching the movie 'Grease' and sleepily singing along. One by one, the singing died down, until I was the last one awake. I glanced at Nina's alarm clock, it was already four a.m. I sighed and forced my eyes closed. But the moment I did, Garrett's shocked expression from earlier, played behind my lids and I giggled quietly to myself.

Kathey Gray

CHAPTER TWELVE

Desire

Garrett's tongue was hot in my mouth and his danced with mine so expertly that I was getting dizzy. His left hand slid underneath my wet hair and held, while his right hand explored, skimming down my body. It slid down my back and dared even lower, groping my bottom. I gasped aloud into his mouth at his brashness.

"Corinne," he moaned. "God, I've waited so long for this to happen."

Unable to even process his words fully, I could only whimper in response. He didn't give me much more time to respond anyway, before his tongue was back in my mouth. *Jesus,* no wonder Garrett always got models into his bed. Who could say no to *this?* Our clothes were sodden by now and normally I would be shivering, if I wasn't aching with heat from that kiss. My mouth felt like it was on fire. My body felt unhinged, like my limbs had gone soft and languid. I couldn't even *believe* the way things were going. An hour ago, I was worried Garrett was going to awkwardly turn me down then avoid me for at least a year before our friendship eventually fizzled away. Garrett finally pulled away, although the heat in his eyes didn't turn down an octave.

"We should probably go now, huh?" He smirked irresistibly.

I cleared my throat. "Uh-huh," I nodded.

He pulled me off of the wall and led me to his sleek car. I was relieved to see that the rain had stopped completely. While concentrating on avoiding the deadly parking lot puddles, my phone rang. I pulled it out of my purse and slid my finger across the shiny new screen.

"Hello?"

"Don't you fucking *dare* sleep with him on the first night! Corinne, have I taught you *nothing?* That man better at least take you on *three* proper dates before you even *consider* that!"

I looked around. "What the? Where *are* you?"

"To the left, behind the grey SUV."

I was amazed to see Roberta sitting in her car. Her white Corvette stuck out in the parking lot well enough.

I whispered into the phone. "What the *hell,* Roberta? Have you been watching us the *whole* time?" My face burned.

"*Yes!* Because you can't be *trusted!* Stay there, I'm pulling around. Tell him *goodbye!*"

"*What?*" I whispered.

But she hung up and began to pull from her spot. Dammit. I think I'd just been *cock blocked!* By my *best* friend!

I shuffled awkwardly in my baby blues. "Um, Garrett?"

By then he had unlocked his car and was opening the door for me. "Yeah?" He smiled irresistibly. *What the fuck was I saying again?*

"Hey, batch! Did you forget about those errands we were supposed to run together?" Roberta shouted out of her car window. Big black shades covered her eyes, partially concealing her entertainment. If it wasn't for her playful grin, I'd probably believe it myself.

"Hey, Garrett," she nonchalantly addressed him, an afterthought.

"Hey... Roberta." Garrett ran his hand up the back of his neck, uneasily. He knew he was busted by the bestie. Guilt was all over his face.

Roberta waited.

I turned to Garrett and shrugged. "Catch you next time?" I asked with a sheepish grin.

"Sure. Yeah, yeah," he agreed immediately, too afraid to go up against Roberta.

I skipped over to hug him and kissed him on his grainy cheek. He blushed even harder then and held me gently in those God awful death machine arms of his for just a moment. I smiled up at him and he smirked with promise back.

Then I turned on wobbly legs and got into Roberta's car. We both waved at Garrett and rode off. Roberta turned to me. "You'll thank me later," she looked at me pointedly.

I sighed. "You're probably right. Things moved pretty quickly. I wasn't really expecting that," I admitted, blushing.

Roberta turned the wheel, nodding. "Well at least you know you two have sexual chemistry. That was one *hot* kiss," she giggled. "Practically steamed up my windows from here," she joked.

I laughed. "Yes, it was."

I sat in silence, recalling it, before dashing out of my memory. "Do we *really* have errands to run?"

Roberta scoffed. "No, but we can go do something if you want?" She offered.

I shook my head. "No, I just want to go to home. I'm all wet." I stared out of the rainy window in a daze.

"I'm sure you *are!*" Roberta teased.

I turned to her with my mouth hanging open and a smile.

"Just promise me you won't touch my vibrator," she laughed.

My jaw felt like it hit the floor. "I don't use a *vibrator!*" I accused in shock.

Roberta slid onto the freeway smoothly, accelerating. She ignored the looks I was giving her. "Well, maybe that's the *problem*, then! We need to get you one, ASAP!" She said, matter-of-factly.

I scoffed. "I do *not* need a vibrator."

She turned to me, arching a brow. "Girl, *everyone* needs a vibrator."

I gave her a weird look before quieting down. I knew there was no point in arguing. She would somehow find a way to buy me one, whether I liked it or not.

* * *

We rode the rest of the ride home listening to Amy Winehouse and the sound of the rain. But of course, I couldn't concentrate on either of those things when all I could think about was Garrett. He invaded my mind and forced fantasy after fantasy in it.

We pulled into our parking garage and parked. I got out feeling less sexy than before. Now my damp clothes felt like a sticky nuisance. We entered the apartment.

"I'm going to take a shower," I informed Roberta.

She nodded and I retreated to the bathroom. I kicked off my soppy heels and unbuttoned the wet dress, shimmying it off. I peeled off my bra and panties and was about to step in, when my phone screen on the bathroom counter lit up with a new message. It was from Garrett. I walked over to it, completely naked.

What are your plans tomorrow?

A thrill ran through me and I fought the urge to jump up and down. I set my phone back down. *He can wait*, I thought smugly. Then I got into the shower and let the hot water rain down on me, washing off all of the sticky lust.

I thought of Garrett again and suddenly wished for a vibrator.

CHAPTER THIRTEEN
Ninth Grade

And just the way I'd found he'd arrived, it was the same way I found out he was leaving. Roberta ran up to me. "Have you heard the news?" She huffed.

I was at my locker, putting away my books. Since I'd gotten to high school, I'd been busy trying to fend off the older boys. Somehow they'd taken notice that I was *female*, and unfortunately that was all the encouragement they needed. That and the fact that any girl that was above a five on the 'hotness Richter scale' was deemed 'fresh meat'. I was a solid seven. I guess the highlights I'd gotten in my hair, made me stand out more, or maybe it was the small curves I'd developed. Roberta was already downright voluptuous by then, and a ten in anyone's eyes. But since word got out that she had a hell of a left hook and wasn't afraid to use it, needless to say, boys were more intimidated by *her*.

"No, what is it?" I asked, shutting my locker.

"Garrett's *moving!*" And as she said it, her own face fell with realization.

My heart felt like it hit the floor and then crawled away, probably to die in a hole somewhere.

"*What?*" My voice was barely above a whisper. I was trying to look anything but devastated, but that's exactly how I felt...*ruined*...*destroyed*.

"His dad got offered a higher paying job in Florida. They're leaving in a few weeks," she informed me.

I felt the crippling ache start to spread inside of me. This had to be a cruel prank that Roberta was playing on me. But it wasn't April Fool's Day, was it?

"You're *joking*, right?" I checked with her.

"I wish," she smiled sadly.

But...but. He can't *leave*. 'He can't just...*leave us here!*' I wanted to scream.

But that's exactly what he did. Two weeks later, Roberta and I stood in Garrett's driveway, saying our goodbyes.

I stared at the U-Haul, packed up with Garrett's family's belongings, feeling sick.

"Guess this is goodbye," Garrett shrugged. He'd always had strength and an amazing ability to hold his composure. He smirked sadly and his slanted eyes were wider and greener than usual.

I nodded and looked away from the honesty of his gaze. Tears welled in my eyes and I blinked them back. Garrett did the polite thing and pretended not to notice.

Roberta, tough as always said, "*wait a minute!* You *said* you were going to call us once a week *and* send us letters, don't forget about *that!*" She reminded him fiercely.

He chuckled. "I guess there's always that," he agreed.

Roberta stepped forward and hugged him first. "Send us some seashells, too!" She smiled sadly.

"For sure," he chuckled.

Roberta pulled back and walked back to her bike, giving me a chance to say goodbye, in private.

"Corinne," he started. "I, um, made you something," Garrett shuffled on his feet.

He pulled a leather corded bracelet from his pocket. A small golden charm hung from it. He picked up my arm, raising it up. He unhooked the cord, and wrapped it around my wrist, fastening it back. I turned my wrist over and inspected the charm.

"It's a moon," Garrett told me. Then he showed me his that he was wearing on his left arm. "I have the sun," he informed me, showing me the matching bracelet.

I felt a strange warm rush run through me followed by a dull ache in my chest. "You *made* this for me?" I asked in disbelief. He nodded and smiled proudly. I shook my head. "Thank you, Garrett," I smiled. I hugged him one last time before joining Roberta, climbing onto my bike as well.

Roberta looked over at me, then back at Garrett. "Hey, *I* didn't get a bracelet!" She complained.

* * *

Garrett kept his promise. He called me and Roberta every Sunday. He also sent letters and bags of seashells every now and then. Roberta and I had a collection in our old clubhouse that we'd still visit every weekend. Still, the year droned on. Life was emptier. Our trio had been broken up and now everything we did, felt a little more hollow than before, *without* Garrett. He was supposed to come visit us next summer, but that seemed lightyears away. Roberta went through boys as fast as she changed outfits. But she never did let things go far. She was saving herself for "the one", for marriage. I knew the feeling. I, too, was saving myself for someone special. Not that I'd ever get to *fulfill* that wish.

I spent a full school year moping around. *How does one get through losing the one you love?* One day at a time. But although Garrett was *alive*, I'd still felt like I'd lost him. Of course time passed painfully slow. I felt like I aged more in that one year than in my whole *life*. But finally it was time for school to let out and for summer to begin.

Roberta and I couldn't wait for our summer adventures together to begin, and for our trio to be reunited once more. We'd already went bathing suit shopping and had both obtained the "perfect" bikinis. We were outside in the backyard, lying on my trampoline, working on our tans, when I got the call. The mood was high, summer was in the air, rock music was playing on the radio, and our lips were stained cherry red from eating popsicles.

"Corinne!" My mom called, poking her head out the back door.

I sat up, nearly going blind from the glare of the sun in my eyes. "What, mom?"

Roberta continued to bounce her feet to the beat of the music with her eyes closed, ignoring us.

"Garrett's on the phone," she yelled, then disappeared back inside, closing the door.

Roberta's eyes popped open and met with mine. She sat up quickly and we both climbed off of the trampoline, squealing. We raced barefoot through the cool grass to the back door. Had he *finally* come? Was it going to be like old times again for a while? Roberta and I fought over the door like fools until we both made it inside, then ran to the phone. I made it there first and picked up the cold receiver in my hand.

"*Hello?*" I breathed.

Roberta fought the receiver out of my hand, until I complied and let her, too, listen by holding it out in between us. We had both of our ears pressed against it.

"*Corinne?* It's Garrett," his voice came on the line.

Roberta and I laughed. "I know, silly. What's up?"

"Roberta's there?" Garrett sounded surprised.

"Yes, of course!" I chirped.

"Hi, Garrett," Roberta chimed in on cue.

"Hey, Roberta..." he answered. But his voice sounded off.

Roberta looked at me funny, like she had heard it, too.

"Why'd you call? Are you *here?* Are you coming *soon?*" I asked eagerly.

There was a pause on the line. Roberta and I continued to stare at each other strangely.

"Garrett, are you there?" Roberta checked.

He sighed heavily on the other line before answering finally. "We're not coming anymore."

CHAPTER FOURTEEN
Skidaway Island

"Of course Garrett had to pick *hiking* for our first date!" I huffed. "He couldn't pick something *normal* and *indoors* like dinner or a movie!" My face flushed.

Knowing my track record, I was imagining all the ways I could humiliate myself in front of him. Garrett was in *excellent* shape, while I was in 'so-so' shape.

"Oh, stop *complaining!* It'll be a fun adventure for you both!" Roberta commented, amused. "If you ask me, it sounds like a *romantic* one, too," she teased, finishing up my braid and wrapping an elastic band around the bottom of it.

I pulled my dark French Dutch braids forward, admiring them. Their soft silk ridges tickled my palms.

"Thanks, these are perfect to keep my hair from frizzing up in the humidity." I stared at my reflection in the full body length mirror at mine and Roberta's apartment. I was wearing ripped up jeans, Converse tennis shoes and a black tank top. I also wore a small backpack on my back containing hiking essentials.

"No prob, girl. Are you wearing 'the' underwear?" Roberta grabbed my shoulders, grinning like a thief in the reflection.

I sighed. "Yes! Although I doubt we're going to be getting it on in the woods." I rolled my eyes.

"You'd be surprised how many people get *wild* in the wild," Roberta winked.

I blushed. "More like get poison ivy," I scoffed.

Roberta ignored me. "You look ready," she encouraged.

"I *look* like Indiana Jones," I huffed.

Roberta rolled her eyes. "More like *Tomb Raider!* You look *hot*, girl. Garrett's going to want to raid your tomb!"

I turned around and gasped. "*Roberta!*" My face was burning red.

"*What?* It's true!" she giggled.

'Knock-knock'

"He's *here!*" Roberta squealed.

I was suddenly glad that my only breakfast was coffee. If I'd ate anything else, it surely would've came up at that moment. I panicked, meeting her eyes. "What if I have to *pee?*"

"*Squat!*" She widened her eyes at me with irritation. She pushed me along, towards the door.

"*Where?*" I asked, frantically.

"In the *bushes*, silly!" She responded, thoroughly exhausted by my ridiculous inquiries.

She was about to open the door, when she paused. "*Oh!* I almost forgot!" She reached beside her to the coat rack where a blue Dodgers baseball cap hung. People always eyed me strangely when I wore it, but I didn't care. My dad had given it to me and that's all that mattered. He was a die hard Dodgers fan, even though we lived in Georgia. She picked it off gingerly and pressed it down on top of my head. "Your hat! You wouldn't want that precious face of yours to get sunburned now, would we?" She baby-talked me.

I shot her a dirty look as she turned the doorknob and flung open the door.

Garrett stood towering in the hallway. He was wearing khaki cargo pants, a tight dri-fit shirt and enormous hiking boots. My eyes followed up his body and met with his eyes. He was smiling the warmest smile at me. It made my nerves begin to dissipate.

"We *match!*" He laughed, pointing at my head. It was that moment that I looked at his too. He was also wearing a blue baseball cap. His was plain without much of a design, but it didn't make it any less funny.

I laughed too, grateful for a shift in the tense atmosphere. My mood had effectively been lightened.

Roberta nodded at me, gloating in her own subtle way.

"Great minds think alike," I shrugged, smiling at Garrett, then turning to wink at Roberta.

Roberta gently pushed me out into the hallway. "You kids have fun now. Garrett, I expect her back in one piece," she warned.

"But of course! You have nothing to worry about!" He insisted.

Roberta nodded. "That's what I like to hear."

We walked out and Roberta shut the door behind her. I was alone with Garrett in the hall. We walked for a few steps in heavy silence, before he reached for my hand. It felt like a lightning bolt shot through it, but I somehow managed to walk with no problems. After we got into his car, a brand spanking new red and black 2018 Camaro. We put down our bags, buckled up, and Garrett sped away.

"So, where to?" I asked.

Garrett turned to me and answered in a resonant voice. "Skidaway Island," he smiled. "Don't worry, it's an easy hike," Garrett reassured me, turning his hat around to wear it backwards.

I nodded.

* * *

I kept quiet through the ride there. I'd never been, but I'd always heard the views were gorgeous.

An hour later, we'd parked and walked to the first trail. The trees were a strange mixture of arched Spanish Moss and Palm. They created a canopy of shade that I was grateful for on this humid day. The ground was sandy and was littered with leaves.

"It's pretty here, I can't believe I've never been," I mentioned as we began walking.

The sunlight shone down through the trees overhead and I watched the shadows dance across Garrett's face. I was mesmerized momentarily, until he answered. "Yes, it is. I can't believe you never have either," he grinned. "I'm also kind of glad you haven't though."

"Why?" I smiled.

"Because the sunsets here are amazing, and I get to be here with you to experience it firsthand," he winked.

I blushed. "Oh...well, good then," I responded, painfully awkwardly.

We walked in silence for a while, just admiring the views and nature. Garrett slowed suddenly, holding out his arm to stop me.

I looked up at his arm and then at him. "What?"

He was staring at something in the trees beyond the trail. He turned to me, drawing his pointer finger across his lips.

"Shhhhhh..." He pointed to the trees in front of us on the left hand side. My heart skipped a little. Deep down I was worried it might be a snake or an alligator. But my body warmed with relief when I saw it was just a baby deer, a fawn. An elated grin spread across Garrett's face.

"*Awwww!*" I whispered.

We both stayed frozen in our tracks, afraid to scare it away.

The fawn watched us cautiously, determining that we wcren't dangerous, before quickly hopping across the trail in front of us and into the trees on the other side.

I let out the breath I'd been holding. "I'm just glad it wasn't a gator!" I finally said.

Garrett chuckled, shaking his head. "Me too!"

After walking and talking for a while, we decided to stop and picnic. We found a rare Spanish Moss tree by itself in a clearing. Garrett slipped off his pack and removed some of the items he'd brought. He laid out a green and blue blanket under the shade. We both sat down and guzzled our water. I flipped off my hat, lying it on the blanket. We got out the snacks that we'd brought, taking them out of our packs. Garrett had brought oat bars and bags of nuts. I had brought apples and pretzels. We snacked and chatted about our jobs and friends for a while. Garrett told me about the software his company was designing. Every time he talked about his work, it just reminded me even more of how brilliant he really was.

We were about to clean up, when I caught Garrett staring at my mouth. We were lying down next to each other and the sun was lowering in the sky. It wasn't quite sunset, but it was drawing near. He reached his hand under my braids, gently wrapping his palm around the back of my neck. His green eyes watched mine intently. I had forgotten how to breathe. He moved closer. "I'm in love with you too, Corinne," he said, in a raw voice.

I didn't know how to respond, hearing him *say* those words aloud was surreal. I'd dreamt of this moment for *years*. It was worth the wait. Garrett closed the distance between us. His warm, soft lips pressed against mine. I kissed him back, losing control and adding my tongue to the occasion. He held my face in his hands and I held his. Before I knew it, he was lying on top of me. Everything was so hot. I felt like I'd temporarily lost consciousness, as his strong body covered mine. He pressed himself onto me and I gasped.

"Seems my body can't help the way I feel, either," he said against my lips, amused.

I giggled. He pulled back to look at me. "You've always been the girl of my dreams, Corinne." He spoke fervently, adding, "and now you're the girl of my fantasies," he murmured.

My mouth fell open and his met with mine once more. His lips went wandering, down my jaw and to my neck. I moaned a little and I heard him groan.

He pulled back, resigned. "We'd better stop before I make love to you in this public park," he shook his head a little, chuckling with an edge. He sat back on his heels.

I laughed on the outside, but on the inside, I was astonished to hear him say those words. It made me melt with desire inside. I sat up. "Yes, we certainly don't want to scare the old grannies and children!" I teased.

His green eyes still swirled with enough desire to make me blush and feel lustful again. "Heaven forbid," he grinned naughtily.

He got up and held his hand out to me. He helped me up, lifting me as if I were a paper doll. We cleaned up our mess and packed away our things. I replaced my blue cap on my head.

We finished our hike until we reached the beach on Tybee Island. We walked in the sand and the water, collecting seashells. Then we sat in the sand and watched the sunset. The clouds were painted across the pink and purple sky.

Garrett held my hand. It was perfect.

CHAPTER FIFTEEN
Tenth Grade

I don't how Roberta and I had managed last summer without Garrett, but we had. Roberta had already started to healthily move on without him, whereas I'd developed a very unhealthy habit of staring at old photos of us every night and replaying old memories in my head. Of course I never told Roberta about it, she'd have thought that was not only weird, but pathetic.

Garrett still called and sent us seashells. But he was also sending us pictures of all the fabulous things he'd been doing in Florida without us. He'd become an avid surfer with the body and tan to match. He did amazing things like swim with dolphins and go snorkeling. Him and his family owned a boat and they took it out frequently. In all his pictures, he couldn't mask the look of pure elation on his features. He loved it there and he was happy. So why couldn't *I* be happy? I was happy for *him*, but didn't he miss us? Didn't he miss...*me?*

I didn't really think life could *get* much worse, and then it did. One day while Roberta and I were shopping, a man approached us. He was dressed sharply and had one of those blindingly celebrity-like smiles. For a moment, I thought he was Tom Cruise. He told us he was a talent scout and thought Roberta would be a perfect fit as a model at his agency. Roberta was flattered, but I was flabbergasted. Of course Roberta was drop dead gorgeous, that was a known fact. But my best friend, a *model?* That would have to vamp up my cool points status about two million points. As excited as *I* was, Roberta handled the man cooly, with a level-headed attitude. She calmly discussed the details of the job as she took his card.

"I'll get back to you," she said, as she shook his hand.

The man walked away and I stood there stunned. Any *other* girl our age would've jumped up and down squealing, thinking they'd just had their lives made for good, but not Roberta. She had a surprisingly mature and realistic view on life for a girl of sixteen.

"That was *amazing!*" I spouted, as soon as the man was out of earshot. "What are you going to do?"

Roberta only shrugged. "Check out his business and see if it's legit. If it is, then I guess I'll see what my parents think."

I had no idea how she could handle the situation with such poise, when inside I felt like someone had let a bouncy ball loose in my brain. She'd acted like it was no big deal, but before I knew it, it became a *major* deal.

* * *

"I'm flying to Milan next week," Roberta casually mentioned at lunch.

I spit out my chocolate milk back into the carton. "*What?*"

She smiled. "They want me to do a few shoots for Cosmo Girl and participate in fashion week," her eyes glowed a little, showing her first sign of real excitement.

"*Holy shit*," I breathed. "Cosmo Girl *magazine?* Fucking *fashion week?* Roberta...you've *made* it!" I beamed.

She finally wriggled in her seat a little, letting out the tiniest squeal. "I know, right? My parents are freaking out, too," she admitted.

I looked around our cafeteria. "Who else knows?"

She raised her eyebrows in warning. "You, my parents and the school. I don't really want anyone else to know right now. If things get crazy here at school then I'll have to switch schools or be home-schooled."

I gasped. "*No!*"

She shook her head. "Exactly."

Next week came and went. Then another, then another. Roberta had been gone for a month, and as much as she tried to keep things a secret, the wings of curiosity had taken flight in our school.

"Corinne, I'm in Paris," Roberta's voice sounded fuzzily from the other line.

"That's amazing," I twirled the phone cord around my finger. "What's it like?"

"The Eiffel Tower is really as awesome as it is in the movies, the hot chocolate is to *die* for and the men are complete *babes*." I could just imagine the sly wink she'd be giving me in person.

"Sounds like a dream," I breathed. "Any idea of when you'll be coming back?"

She sighed, dismayed. "Probably another month. They want to keep me here for more shoots and introduce me to the European crowd and all that jazz," she said in her nonchalant way.

"Oh," my voice fell.

"I miss you, best friend!" She suddenly chimed. "Did you get my package yet?"

I stared down at the opened package in my hand, containing a post card from Milan, an Eiffel Tower keychain, and a fuzzy white beret hat. "I did. Thank you," I answered. I had no idea where I'd wear *that* hat to, but what I *really* wanted was my best friend back.

"Okay, well I gotta go. I'll call you next week! I love you! Ciao, Bella!"

"Love you too," I said before the line cut off.

* * *

Months went by like that before the news broke. I had just gotten to school that day and sat in my seat. The boys in the class were passing around a magazine and snickering. I ignored them at first, but they just wouldn't quit. So when the boy behind me got his turn to hold the magazine, I turned around to see what the fuss was about. My mouth fell open when my eyes fell upon *my* best friend, Roberta, wearing only a red bikini, high heels and jewels around her neck. Her long dark hair was slicked down her back and she carried a designer purse as she looked off into the distance, smiling, seemingly focused at someone just past the lens. After the initial shock wore off, it was replaced by anger.

"*Give* me *that!*" I growled, snatching the magazine.

The boy looked like he was about to argue, his face turned red with anger, until he saw my cutting glare. I turned back around and shut the magazine. It was the latest issue of Vogue. My heart stopped as I realized I might be losing my friend for good.

Word spread like wildfire after that. Roberta was now known as "that chick who does modeling."

People had even started to pester *me* about it. Boys would ask me for her number and girls would ask me to talk to her for them, to see if she could help them get into modeling. It was really annoying.

So I wasn't surprised when I got the call. "Corinne? My parents said I can't go back to school. I have to do homeschool," Roberta sighed.

CHAPTER SIXTEEN

Withholding

On the drive back from Skidaway Island, I suddenly had questions for Garrett. They flooded my mind all at once.

"Um, Garrett?"

He glanced over at me. "What is it?" He knew by the tone of my voice that something was amiss.

"Why didn't you *tell* me? If you felt the same way...?" I was almost afraid to ask, since we'd had such a perfect day. But the curiosity was beginning to eat at me.

He was silent for a moment, staring at the dark road ahead. He sighed before answering. "The same reason *you* didn't tell *me*. I'd always wondered, in the back of my mind, if you saw me as more than a friend. But...I just couldn't risk it." His eyes flashed to mine for a moment, naked with vulnerability. "I know that makes me a coward," he admitted with a crooked smile.

"No more a coward than me," I huffed.

He smiled broader, with more confidence, before he went on. "You're my best friend, Corinne. I would *never* try to jeopardize that," he glanced over at me with a sweet smirk. He looked back to the road. "I would never risk losing you. But when I got your text, well...it was all the push I *needed* to pursue what I've always *wanted*..."

I felt my breath catch in my throat. I didn't have to ask what it was he wanted, because his eyes slid over to mine.

"*You*."

How can *one* word hold so much *magnitude?* The intensity of his gaze made my heart pound in my chest. He was just as besotted with me, as I was with him? But *how?* I was freed of the hypnotic spell he had me under, when he turned forward to stare at the road once more. It took me a full five minutes of silence before I could speak again.

"So...*all* those other women...?" I raised my eyebrows.

Garrett scoffed. "What *about* them?"

"Well...were those relationships not *serious?*" I prodded.

"Far from," he shook his head adamantly. "The closest thing I had to serious was what I had with Annette. But even then, something felt incomplete. I wish I'd known what the missing feeling meant before. Now I know."

Just when I thought he couldn't woo me more, he did.

"You can't give away something that's already taken," he winked at me.

"Oh," I croaked.

We'd arrived in my neighborhood and shortly after, we were outside of mine and Roberta's apartment. We parked and Garrett ran to open my door. I stifled a giggle, it was just so *weird*. He held his hand out for mine and pulled me out of the car, shutting the door behind him. He locked his car before we headed inside and up the elevator. We walked down the hall and to the door of the apartment. I suddenly felt incredibly shy. I stared at Garrett's shoes. His feet were ginormous, they'd always been. A low warning in the back of my mind reminded me of what that meant, the whole "big feet" myth, and I blushed unnecessarily.

"That was...an amazing date. Thank you, Garrett."

"It was...it was amazing." Garrett's deep, focused voice dipped down low, causing me to look up.

There was that intensity again. There was that look. That heart-pounding, chill-raising, panty-dropping, knee-weakening look. That look that said 'I can fuck up your world in ways you can't even imagine.' My lips parted accordingly and Garrett pushed me back against the door. His mouth met with mine, roughly and needing. I felt like I was falling. Oh no, wait...I was *actually* falling. I stumbled backward into Roberta, who caught me and righted me. Garrett just barely caught himself before falling onto his face. Roberta stared at me and Garrett in shock, her mouth hanging open. I couldn't believe that we'd stunned *Roberta* into silence! That had be to some kind of *record!* She glared at us in silent disapproval.

"Goodnight, Garrett," she said, before swiftly shutting the door in his face. I caught the wolfish grin he was wearing just before the door closed.

"*Goodnight, Corinne!*" He yelled through the door.

I giggled, covering my mouth quickly after catching Roberta's ruffled stare.

She was wearing pink cat pajamas, her dark silky hair was in a messy bun and she held a glass of red wine in her hand. She arched a groomed eyebrow at me. "I'm assuming that went *well?*"

I chuckled deeply and indulgently.

"Want some wine?" She held her glass up.

"Always," I nodded.

She walked into our kitchen and I followed. I watched her pour wine into a glass for me. She handed it to me and I sipped on it, welcoming the sweet taste and warming effect it had on my body.

"Let's sit and talk about your first date with Garrett!" She skipped cheerfully, her sour mood from seconds earlier had all but vanished.

I laughed a little. "Okay."

We sat in our living room. Roberta had the lights turned low and some candles lit. Soulful music from her playlist swayed softly in the background. I set my phone down on the coffee table as we each took a seat in the leather seats opposite of each other.

I replayed mine and Garrett's date for her, trying to ignore the humongous grin she'd had when I told her about our scaldingly hot make-out sesh on our picnic and our heated conversation in the car.

"Wow—I'm *proud* of you Corinne!" She smiled, her eyes twinkling.

"For what?" I sipped my wine.

"For not giving him the 'v' yet! Sounds like he was trying to charm your pants right off!" She laughed.

"He *was!*" I laughed too. "But I think you were right. We need to take this slow. If not..." I shook my head. "It'll all blown up in our face."

Roberta shook her head. "No, you don't want that to happen," she agreed. "So, when are you seeing him again?"

I shrugged and sipped my wine again. "No idea."

My phone on the table buzzed and both of our eyes snapped to it.

"Is that *him?*" She waggled her eyebrows at me, smiling naughtily.

"I don't know..." I muttered, reaching forward and picking up the phone.

I slid the phone screen over and saw the contact name. I bit my lip.

"It's him, isn't it?" Roberta asked in a knowing voice.

"Yessss..." I fought my shameless smile back by tugging my bottom lip down with my teeth.

"What is he saying?"

I raised my eyebrows and met her eyes. "He wants a second date," I breathed. "He's asking when I'm free."

"Of *course* he does, that horn-dog!" She laughed. "You better go buy some condoms, and fast!"

My mouth fell open and a furious flush spread onto my cheeks.

"But I'm withholding the 'v', remember?" I laughed.

"Honey, with the way you guys kissed on our front door..." she trailed off, sipping her wine, then met my eyes again. "You need to be prepared for *anything.*"

I nodded, then remembered suddenly. "Hey, Roberta...do you believe in that myth, the whole big feet...?" I trailed off unable to finish.

She caught onto my implication easily. "Big 'd'?" She winked. "*Completely.* That's not a myth, it's a science."

"I'm in trouble then, aren't I?" I breathed.

A huge grin plastered on her face and her head fell back, eyes on the ceiling. "*Loads*."

CHAPTER SEVENTEEN
Eleventh Grade

With Roberta being homeschooled and jet-setting across the country, I was left completely alone. Garrett still kept in touch, but not like he used to. He was starting to move on. He was starting to forget about us...starting to forget about *me*. I moped around like a ghost haunting the school. I felt like *nobody* noticed me. Until one day, somebody *did*.

I was sitting at my desk during English class, doodling on notebook paper in my spiral, when someone's voice interrupted my daydream. "Who's Garrett?"

My head snapped up and my heart jumped in my chest. It was a boy that sat in the back of the class. He was kind of quiet and usually had earbuds in. He was of average height with brown hair that seemed to stand straight up. His warm brown eyes seemed friendly enough and his body language was relaxed and inviting, but I still didn't trust him. My face flushed with heat and my eyes flashed with anger. "*Nobody*," I said, covering up the doodle with Garrett's name in the center.

He raised his eyebrows doubtfully, but didn't push it. "So, what's your problem lately?" He set a hand down on my desk and leaned into it. I scooted far away from him in my seat.

"What do you *mean?*" I snapped. My eyes bounced around the room to see if we had an audience, but everyone was too engrossed in their own sources of entertainment to care. Even our teacher was reading a book and listening to classical music during our "quiet time".

"I mean, I don't know you *well*, but I *do* notice you since we're in the same class and all. These last few months, I don't think you've asked *one* question, or spoke much for that matter," he pointed out. "You're not thinking about...like committing suicide, or shooting up the school or anything, right?" He asked, jokingly.

My jaw fell open. "Of *course* not!" I was appalled by his question.

The kid sitting behind me got up, leaving the seat open. The boy moved to sit in it quickly, sliding in like a smooth bandit. I turned around, annoyed. He tapped me on the shoulder and I whirled around.

"*What?*"

"So, that Garrett fellow isn't your boyfriend, is he?"

"I don't think that's any of your business," I huffed.

He leaned back in his chair. "That means no," he chuckled.

When I only gave him a dirty look instead of an answer, he nodded like he knew he was right.

"I'm Eddie," he held out his hand.

I looked at his hand and back up at him. "Corinne," I said, turning back around.

"Well, Corinne, are you busy this weekend? I have two tickets to a Blink 182 concert and my best friend just bailed on me," he said to my back.

I turned around slowly. "Did you say Blink 182?"

He nodded and grinned.

* * *

So, I did something very uncharacteristic for me. I trusted a stranger. Okay, so that's not really fair—I knew Eddie, sort of. I was 95% sure he wasn't a serial killer, anyway. So you can imagine the shock my parents felt when he came to pick me up in his beige El Camino.

"It's great to meet you, Mr. and Mrs. P. You have nothing to worry about— the concert is only forty-five minutes away and it'll be over in *plenty* of time for Corinne to be home for her eleven o'clock curfew," he'd said.

My parents seemed skeptical of our sudden friendship, but for some reason they still let me go. Maybe they also felt sorry for me. Had I been *that* transparent?

I'd went with Eddie, not only because I loved Blink 182 and knew I'd never get another chance at free tickets, but because I had nothing to lose. I'd already lost *both* of my best friends. I needed a *new* friend.

I had a surprisingly good time with Eddie that night and we began to hang out more often. But instead of swimming, riding bikes and getting ice cream, we'd visit vintage music stores and open mic nights. Eddie was crazy about music and played the drums for a band called 'Set Me Apart'. The first time I went to watch him play, I was surprised at the feeling it gave me. Eddie was a different person when he played...wild, uninhibited and passionate. I'd felt attracted to him for the first time. After that, things changed. Eddie started holding my hand when we'd go out. We talked on the phone for longer. We'd share the same straw when we'd get shakes. And after we'd had our first kiss at one of our open mic night dates, he asked me to be his girlfriend. I couldn't very well say no, we spent almost every day together. And the idea of *belonging* to someone did *sound* nice.

But a tiny part of me was sad when he kissed me. The first thing I'd thought when he did was, 'I was saving that for Garrett.'

* * *

We'd been dating for a year when I lost my virginity to Eddie, the summer of my jr. year. I hadn't planned for it to go that way, we'd just gotten caught up in the heat of moment. Deep down, I'd always fantasized about Garrett being my first, as impossible as it seemed. I knew it wasn't a realistic thought. I'd told myself I'd finally let go of him, grown up and moved on. Maybe Eddie would never be *Garrett*, but he cared about me to no end. We'd even said the dreaded 'L' word to each other.

I thought I'd moved on, until one day Eddie asked when we were lying in his bed together after making love, "why do you always wear this bracelet?" He lifted up my arm to inspect it. The tiny gold charm dangled and he caught it in his fingers. "Does it mean something special?" He smiled.

It was like he poked my heart with a stick. I pulled my arm away. "What do you *mean?* It's just a *bracelet*," I snapped defensively.

He found my annoyance endearing. "But you never take it off," he continued.

He was right. And I *would* never. That's when I realized I still wasn't over Garrett Simmons. No matter how much I loved Eddie. No matter how many days and nights, or months and years we spent together, I'd always be waiting on Garrett in the end.

No matter how much I hated to admit it. I'd always be saving a special part of me for him. A part that no one else could ever touch or reach.

CHAPTER EIGHTEEN
New River Trail

I'd worked all week with Roberta and the weekend was finally here. I was still washing the sand out of my hair from my last date with Garrett, and he was about to take me out for our next date. He wouldn't tell me what we were doing, but he did say he was going to pick me up early on Saturday morning. I had my condoms packed safely away in my purse in case the unthinkable happened. Garrett had told me to dress 'sporty'. So I knew we'd be doing something active, and with Garrett, that could mean *anything*.

"He's so crazy..." I shook my head, drinking my coffee, sat next to Roberta at our coffee bar in the kitchen.

"He's *Garrett*," she nodded. "You knew this about him," she pointed out.

I sighed. "I know...but in my defense, he did get crazier after he lived in Florida."

She tilted her head to the side. "True. At least you know he's going to be a hellcat in bed," she clinked her mug against mine.

I lifted my mug to my lips. "Hmm..."

I didn't really know what to say to that. The idea of sleeping with Garrett was scarier to me than *any* adventure he planned to take me on.

Her phone lit up with a message and a little smirk appeared on her full lips.

"What's *that* about?" My lips twitched.

"*Nothing!* Okay, well it is *something*. It's this guy from my past and he's been begging me to give us another go," she admitted, staring at her phone.

"*Really?*" I asked, interested. "He hot?"

"*Yesssss...*" She admitted, blushing. "He's super fucking hot."

"So, what happened? Back then?"

"We were younger then and both not ready for a serious relationship," she sighed, reminiscing.

I nodded. "And things have changed *now?*"

She sipped her coffee, her blue eyes holding mine. "I mean, yeah. I've been thinking about what it would be like to have someone, to settle down. Now that my modeling career is slowing down. It'd be nice, you know?"

"You're only twenty-two, Roberta," I reminded her.

She giggled. "I'm old fashioned! And he was really sweet..."

"Let me see, where's his picture?" I held my free hand out.

She pressed the screen a few times then slid the phone over.

"Yup, I'd give that a second chance too. What the hell, Roberta? Is he a model, too?"

She chuckled. "Yes."

There was a knock at the door and our eyes met. Mine with panic and hers with excitement.

"That'll be my date," I rose. I walked around to the sink and placed my mug in it. Then I made my way back to the front door.

Roberta sat, still in her pajamas. "Have fun..." she sang. Her phone lit up with another message and her head snapped to it, she giggled immediately after.

"You too," I called, smirking.

I opened the door and there was Garrett, dressed in rugged pants, a t-shirt and tennis shoes. But the thing that stood out the most, was the helmet he had strapped on his head. I furrowed my eyebrows at him, as he handed me a helmet.

"Hint-hint," he smiled.

When we got outside, I found two mountain bikes strapped to the back of a bike rack, on a very shiny bright ocean blue Jeep Wrangler.

I looked at Garrett. "Whose is *that?*"

His lips quirked up. "I had a friend who owed me a favor."

"So we're going biking then?" A grin spread across my face.

Garrett walked over to the passenger door and nodded once with an irresistibly boyish smile. "We're going biking." He opened the door for me and I climbed in, placing the helmet on my lap.

In no time he was climbing into the driver's seat and starting up the engine. "Ever been to New River Trail?" He flashed me cheeky grin.

"Of course not," I scoffed. Truth be told, it had been forever since I'd biked at all. But I had missed it. It used to be one of my favorite things to do...one of *our* favorite things to do.

Approximately 30 minutes later, we had arrived. We got out and Garrett took the bikes off the rack, one by one. I tried to look like I wasn't paying attention to his strong hands and rippling, muscled, vascular arms, but I probably failed. Garrett was polite enough not to tease me about checking him out.

"Ready?" He smiled, as soon as the bikes were on the ground. I noticed he'd brought his pack again and I was grateful. I had forgotten mine today.

I nodded, watching as Garrett climbed onto his bike. I climbed onto mine, still holding the helmet awkwardly.

"Nu-uh, you have to wear you helmet, too," he chuckled.

Heat flooded my cheeks as I slipped it on and fastened it under my chin.

"See? You look so cute," he winked, slipping on his dark sunglasses.

I blushed even harder, deciding to slip on my own pair of sunglasses to hide my face. We started off on the trail and I was already in a state of bliss. Although it was humid, there was a slight breeze blowing back my hair. Tall trees towered over either side of us, that gave way into lush forests. We passed over bridges and past soggy fields. We barely spoke, so enchanted by our ride. Mud coated our tires and flung upwards, spraying us like paint. We both laughed when we realized how dirty we were.

"*Great* date, Garrett," I teased sarcastically, gesturing to my clothes.

He laughed. "Sorry, I guess I didn't think you'd mind getting a little muddy." He wiped his hand off on his own pants off. "Or a lot muddy."

We laughed again, even harder.

"I guess we're not going to eat at a fancy restaurant after this, huh?" I joked.

"No, I saved that for our next date," he smiled.

"Oh?" I asked, stunned. "You already planned our next date?"

He nodded. "I did."

I perched atop my bike, straddling it. "And what makes you think I was going to agree to that?" I asked with my hands on my hips.

He laughed, blushing. "Well, I was hoping you would, anyway. It's at The Olde Pink House? I made reservations."

My jaw dropped and I had to tell my brain pick it back up. "For *when?*"

"Next Saturday?" His face pinched up. "Is that okay?"

I tried not to overreact, but The Olde Pink House was not only one of Savannah's most well known and favorite restaurants, it also had an expensive reputation.

"Sure, that'll be fine," I shrugged, playing it off. Relief fell over his features. "Hey, Garrett?"

"Yes?"

"Race 'ya?" I challenged before taking off, without awaiting his answer.

I heard him laughing behind me, then swiftly mounting his bike and racing on my tail.

CHAPTER NINETEEN
Twelfth Grade

Eddie and I broke up right before senior year started. It was a mutual thing. We didn't have that 'forever' kind of love and we both knew it. He started dating a girl named Serenity who was also a guitarist in her own girl band. They were better suited for each other. We didn't harbor any bad blood for each other, though. In a way, I was thankful to him for getting me through the eleventh grade. But isn't it the way of fate. As soon as you feel like you're over someone for good, they come marching right back into your life.

I was walking into my new Science class for the first time, when my heart stopped beating in my chest for three seconds. It was *Garrett*. He was sitting at a desk that he scarcely fit into. He was even more striking than the last time I saw him. His skin had gained color and his hair had lightened from years in the sun. His green eyes found mine and he hopped up immediately. His long legs paced over to me quickly and he wrapped me into a tight bear hug. "*Corinne!*" He said warmly. His voice had deepened considerably and it rumbled through me.

"Garrett," I gasped. "What are you *doing* here?"

My heart was racing so fast, I felt like I couldn't breathe. Inside, I was panicking. *He still can't have this control over me, can he?* I worried to myself.

He pulled back and stared down at me. "I wanted to surprise you," he admitted, his voice like honey.

I glanced around to see every other girl in class staring daggers at me. I gulped and returned my eyes to his. "Well you *did!* So what are you doing back now?" I smiled. 'Don't get excited, don't get your hopes up,' my subconscious whispered cautiously. *Too fucking late*, I thought.

"Yeah! My family's moved back. They wanted me to finish my senior year where I grew up," he shrugged adorably and flashed me a broad smile.

"That's nice of them," I said absentmindedly, lost in my own head.

I had mixed emotions about his return. It's what I wished for, what I *prayed* for, for years. But *now,* I didn't know if I could *handle* all of the feelings he'd bring out in me. Feelings of desire, longing, and desperate infatuation— they overwhelmed me when he was around. And now that he was...let's face it, a *man*, things would only be multiplied tenfold. Could I *handle* that kind of devastation again?

Garrett leaned forward and asked in a lower voice. "Are you not *happy* to see me?" He blinked rapidly. "I thought you'd be happy..." he couldn't hide the disappointment in his voice. The smile erased from his mouth.

"Garrett, I couldn't be *happier*," I murmured fervently, meeting his eyes, before pulling him back into a deep hug.

"Good. I am too," he mumbled into my hair.

"Alright, you two," came the teacher's voice. "Break it up and take a seat," he commanded.

My face was already burning as we pulled away. I hid my face with my hair. Garrett sat down and patted the seat in front of him. "I saved it for you," he informed me. But something caught my eye. Garrett was wearing the same matching black corded bracelet, with the matching sun charm to my moon. A wave of heat ran through my body. His eyes followed mine and then fell to my left arm, where my bracelet still remained.

"Thanks," I mumbled, sitting.

I turned around and pretended to un-see it. After a few beats of awkward silence, he spoke up.

"Still have yours, huh?" He whispered.

Chills ran down my spine.

"I never take mine off," he admitted.

I stared at the teacher's back as he talked, hearing nothing he said.

I turned a little, so that only the profile of my face showed. "Me either," I admitted, with a shy smirk.

My face burned and I swear I could feel his burning behind me. I didn't dare turn around to check.

We both pretended to pay strict attention to our new teacher for at least thirty minutes before attempting to talk again. I felt Garrett's fingers tap gently on my shoulder.

"Psst— where's Roberta? I haven't seen her anywhere."

I rolled my eyes and whispered over my shoulder. "Home school."

"*What?*" He whisper yelled.

"It's a long story," I turned and muttered quietly.

* * *

At lunch, I filled Garrett in on Roberta's absence. He admitted he knew she'd been modeling, but didn't know how big she'd gotten.

"Well, that's crazy," he shook his head.

"Isn't it?" I agreed.

All day long I'd been trying to calm down my smile, worried I'd look like a lunatic to him, but it was hard. My cheeks were hurting so bad from trying to hold it in. But I couldn't help it. He made me so *happy*. He was back and every moment spent with him felt like it was cut out of a golden space in time. We could talk about something as boring as the weather and he'd somehow make it interesting. I'd be left hanging onto his every word, his every motion like always. How could I pretend to be anything *less* than fascinated? That's what the *real* problem was with Garrett, I lost track of time. As soon as he was gone, all I did was wait for my next chance to be with him.

He was my worst distraction and my favorite obsession.

"So, what are you doing after school?" He asked me.

"Working," I cringed.

"You have a *job* now? How *long* have I been gone?" He put his hands on his head dramatically.

I giggled. A huge grin stretched across his face. His eyes shined.

"God, I've missed you, Corinne," he admitted.

I blushed so hard, I had to look away for a minute. "I've missed you back," I breathed, nodding. *More than you know.*

"So, where do you work?" He asked.

Shit. Dammit. Mother-fucking shit stick.

I didn't want to tell him that I worked at the same ice cream shop that we frequented as kids! *How embarrassing!*

"I...uh—"

My phone buzzed. "Hold that thought," I held up my finger.

I looked down at my phone. "Holy shit!" I squeaked.

"What?" Garrett asked.

"Roberta's in town!" I enthused.

Garrett smiled warmly. "The three musketeers reunited."

I smiled so hard it hurt.

CHAPTER TWENTY
Dirty Love

After a muddy bike riding adventure, we headed back to the Jeep. We had both crashed a few times, I had the scrapes and bruises to prove it. Garrett fared better than me and helped me back up each time I fell. By the end of the day, we had laughed so hard that my stomach hurt from it, and we were dirty enough to pass for farmhands. Garrett strapped the dirty bikes onto the back of the Jeep, then turned to face me. He covered his mouth with a muddy hand at the sight of me.

"*What?* I know I look like 'Carrie' just swap the pig's blood for mud," I joked.

He stepped closer, his smile fading.

"That's what you were thinking, wasn't it?" I checked, my voice raising an octave from the steadily increasing look of lust in Garrett's eyes.

I backed up until my back hit the side of the Jeep and still he stepped closer, looking at our feet for a moment. The top of his head was almost touching my nose.

"No," he answered, shaking his head, his voice rolling in grit. He lifted his eyes to mine. "I was thinking about how good you look dirty."

Out of any *other* human male's mouth, those words would've sounded extremely corny and mildly offensive. But out of *Garrett's* well mannered, polite mouth, they were exceptionally *hot*.

"I—um, *thanks?*" I laughed, awkwardly. "You look pretty great dirty...too..." The last part of my sentence was lost in a breathy whisper as Garrett leaned down and moved in to kiss me. Every nerve ending in my body awakened as his mouth covered mine. I closed my eyes and felt his hands push my palms against the Jeep. He had me pinned, trapped in a thick haze of passion. I was at his mercy in every way. *I wonder if he knew that?* His mouth took command of mine and we kissed until I was dizzy and no longer aware of anything around us. I was barely able to hold myself up afterwards. My knees felt so weak, I thought they'd give out.

He pulled back, his eyebrows knitting together. "We should go."

I nodded. Then he added with a sigh, "Roberta's going to *kill* me."

I giggled and he chuckled, because it was true.

"What about your friend? Is he going to kill us for muddying up his Jeep?" I wondered aloud.

Garrett shrugged. "The seats are leather and he owes me too big to say anything to me about it."

I felt my eyebrows creep up on my face. "If you say so," I said skeptically.

* * *

We got in and drove back to mine and Roberta's apartment. I opened the door with Garrett standing behind me. Roberta jumped a least a foot backwards upon sight of us, spilling her glass of wine.

"What the *fuck*, Corinne? You scared the *hell* out of me!" She accused.

Garrett and I laughed.

"I know, I'm sorry. I know we look like mud monsters," I admitted.

Roberta marched over to Garrett. "What the *hell* did you do to her?" She pointed in his face, fighting a grin.

Garrett was already smiling so big, I knew she wouldn't stay mad for long. It was an extremely hard thing to do, staying mad at Garrett, that is. He just had one of those extremely lovable, charming personalities. It was irresistible. Just then, a piece of dried mud fell from Garrett's smiling cheek, onto the floor and crumbled into pieces. Roberta followed the motion with her eyes and her mouth fell open. The dried mud had landed on her favorite red, Persian rug. Her head snapped back to him and she narrowed her eyes. Garrett's eyes grew wide.

She pointed at him. "You—*out!*" She commanded.

He backed up immediately the way he came. "Bye, Corinne! See you next weekend!" He waved goofily.

I bit down on the pad my dirty thumb, smiling. "Bye, Garrett."

As soon as he was out of sight, Roberta swung the door closed and set to work cleaning up our trail of mud and mopping up her wine spill. I cringed a little.

"Sorry, Roberta," I apologized.

"It's okay," she huffed. "I'm glad you guys had good dirty fun...now get your ass in the shower!" She laughed.

I saluted her and did just that. In the shower, I watched the mud swirling down around my toes, smiling like an idiot. Only *Garrett* could drag me through the mud (literally) and I'd still have the best time. I changed into my matching cat pajamas and sat by Roberta on the couch. There was already a glass of white wine waiting for me.

"Thanks." I sipped on it and she nodded.

"Want to watch a movie?" She asked me.

I was glad that her earlier annoyance with me had all but disintegrated.

"Sure, yeah," I immediately agreed.

The tiniest suspicion whispered into my brain, but I waved it off.

"How about 'Mamma Mia'?" She asked.

"Ooo yes! I *love* that movie!"

Roberta was giddy and squealed. "Okay!" She said, decidedly.

We were on the opening scene of Amanda Seyfried singing, when something caught my eye. It was a shiny pair of shoes by the front door. *Men's* shoes. *Had those been there before?* Another thing instantly alarmed me. Roberta was *quiet*, much too quiet.

I turned to her. "Roberta...is someone *here?*"

Her eyes remained on the movie and she sipped her wine, pretending to be engrossed. "What?"

"Why are there *men's shoes* by the door? Is someone *here?*" I repeated, an ever-growing grin working its way onto my face.

Her eyes darted to mine and then back to the screen. "Those are for a modeling shoot," she answered coolly.

I raised a brow. "A *modeling* shoot?" I questioned. "Those are *way* too big for you," I pointed out. "And they're way too manly, too."

Her eyes found mine again and she shrugged. "They're going for that whole androgynous look. I don't know, apparently it's really in right now."

I made a weird face at her, but turned back to the TV. "O—kay."

Not even a minute later, I heard a crash, and me and Roberta both turned. A half naked man covered in tattoos stood in the kitchen, frozen beside the where stack of empty coffee containers, that were to be recycled once stood. They were now scattered all over the floor. His body was tan and superb, jet black hair hung into his dark eyes and an apologetic grin graced his perfect mouth. No doubt about it, this was the model flame from Roberta's past.

Roberta sighed, smiling. "Corinne, this is Rodney, Rodney, Corinne."

CHAPTER TWENTY-ONE
Fortune Teller

Senior year flew by. I had so much fun with Garrett and Roberta, who was in town more often now. She'd been home-schooled, but we still managed to make time for each other. I'd had so much *fun* that I didn't take Garrett leaving again into serious consideration. He was going back to Florida to attend college. My way of dealing with it, was pretending like it wasn't really going to happen.

But the day came that we had to say goodbye yet again. Suddenly, I panicked. *What if this was really it?* He was an adult now, he didn't need his parents anymore. He could meet a girl and get married and *never* return! He could get settled there! What was left for him in Georgia, anyway? Little 'ol *me?*

"Here we are again," he said, his face drawn.

I nodded and much to my dismay, a shudder racked my chest.

"Don't cry, Corinne," he soothed me, sliding his palm from the top of my head, down the length of my hair. "This isn't a forever goodbye," he reassured me.

I sniffed. "Isn't it, though?"

Why was I letting him slip through my fingers again? Why had I wasted all this time *not* telling him? Where had all the time *went?* Every time I thought the moment was perfect, I'd find a reason to push it back. Now here I was, there was *no* more time left to push it back. He was *leaving*. High school was *over* with. *This was it.* This was my *last* chance to tell him and yet like an idiot, I still couldn't force the words out.

He held me in his arms and I held it all in. I felt it building inside of me. The words were on the tip of my tongue. But I swallowed them down like the coward I was.

"Never a forever goodbye," he muttered into my hair.

* * *

After Garrett left, life went back into feeling like a numb existence. I started college in Savannah along with Roberta, who wanted a back-up plan for whenever her modeling career expired.

"It's bound to happen," she had implored to me. "Models peak in their teens."

People handled Roberta's fame more maturely in college. Most were surprised she'd stuck around Georgia instead of going somewhere more prestigious and out of state. But she insisted she only wanted a practical education. I'd started seeing a guy named Phil in one of my classes, and things had begun to get serious.

"He asked me to move in with him after college," I'd told Roberta one day.

She gawked at me. "You aren't *serious?*"

I shrugged. "What's so *wrong* with that?"

"Do you even *love* him?" She accused me critically.

"*Of course!*" I answered too quickly. "...In my way," I added, sheepishly. "He's practical," I defended him.

Roberta's face appeared to be more condescending by the minute.

* * *

For spring break Roberta and I decided to take a quick girls' trip to New Orleans. We visited the House of Blues, ate beignets and roasted alligator, and took haunted tours. We were having the best time and had been out on the streets late one night, when we passed a psychic's studio.

"Let's go *in!*" Roberta urged. "I've *always* wanted to have my fortune told!" She added.

I'd always been leery of places like that, and being in a place known for voodoo and haunted histories only made me feel even more spooked. But if I was being honest, the thing that scared me the most was what I knew a psychic would tell me. It's something I knew deep down in my gut. That feeling that never subsided. *Love.* I knew she'd pick up on it and rat me out. I didn't want *anyone* to know my secret, least of all a *stranger!*

I stared at the glowing neon lights and door beads glinting in the lights reflection. "I don't know, Roberta. These things are always a scam," I argued nervously.

My reflection in the glass was tinged in violet and it seemed to mock me.

"I *know!*" She scoffed. "But it'll be *fun!*" She insisted, grabbing my hand and dragging me along.

"It's probably closed," I pulled back on my hand.

But like a bad omen, she pulled on the door with her free hand and it opened, a bell jingling to announce our entrance. At first no one came, and I pulled on her hand again. "Let's go, no one's even here," I complained.

"Can I help you?" Came a voice from the dark hall.

The small dark woman stepped forward. She was wearing a lavender bandanna with swirly gold designs and stars. Her long dark hair was rolled into dreadlocks pulled behind her in a low ponytail that was barely being contained by a thin rubber band. She wore a long white dress and wooden beads around her neck. She was barefoot and the place reeked strongly of incense and marijuana.

Roberta and I remained silent and motionless, so the woman spoke first. "I'm Sonya, you're here to have your fortunes told?" She asked with keen dark eyes.

"Yes," Roberta said. "That's exactly why we're here." She stepped forward.

Sonya nodded. "*You* first," she pointed at me and I gulped.

Roberta had asked me if I felt comfortable doing so, and I insisted it was fine. I didn't want her to know that I'd rather her not hear my fortune be told. She waited for me in the small waiting room while I followed Sonya.

"Take a seat," Sonya urged, after we'd passed through another set of door beads.

I sat down at the small round table and she sat across from me. The room was shrouded with darkness. Incense was lit, along with pink and purple lights in the corners of the room. The walls were painted a strange burnt orange color and were over-textured with bumps. Shelves piled almost to the ceiling with papers, and books lined the walls. The whole room felt suffocating and the thickly scented air only intensified the feeling. To make matters worse, Sonya reached down beside her, grabbing another bottle and lit the incense fuse in that one as well, setting it between us. She coughed right after and waved some of the scent around the room.

I watched her in silence as she took out a set of cards and shuffled them around. Then she splayed them down in front of me, sliding them around and selecting out a few. They all had strange pictures and symbols on them.

"Ah! There are *good* things in the cards for you!" She exclaimed, and I let out a breath.

"That's good," I nodded. *Make it quick*, I thought. I couldn't wait to leave this seedy place.

"You will prosper with your career and I see a friendship. A sisterhood with solid bonds. This is a lifelong friendship," she said, looking down at the cards.

Roberta, I thought, smiling to myself.

"I also see a love," her eyebrows quirked up. "A *great* one, a very *strong* connection," she looked up at me.

"Phil," I accidentally blurted out his name.

"Who's this *Phil?*" She asked.

"My boyfriend, we attend college together," I nodded.

She stared at me for a long time, her eyes probing into mine, examining me closely. Then she shook her head decidedly. *"No."*

I furrowed my eyebrows at her, confused.

"May I?" She gestured to my hand.

I nodded hesitantly, letting her take my right hand in her bony ones, turning my palm over. She studied the lines, tracing them with her rough fingers.

"This love, it will last a lifetime. This love was written in the stars for you. This man is the sun to your moon," she looked up at me, her eyes glinting with mischief.

I felt my heart stop in my chest with a resounding thud. Her words hit me hard with realization. My mouth fell open. A proud wide grin stretched across her thin lips, wrinkling her face.

"The *sun* to your *moon*," she repeated, as her right hand released mine and moved to touch the charm on my bracelet that remained on my left wrist.

CHAPTER TWENTY-TWO

The Olde Pink House

The Olde Pink House stood before me as Garrett opened the door, reaching for my hand. As soon as the door opened, I could hear music playing outside of the restaurant doors. Garrett's large rough palm wrapped gently around mine. His hands were permanently calloused from years and years of lifting weights. Warm light poured onto the sidewalk, inviting us inside. My deep emerald cocktail dress shimmered in the light. Roberta and I had shopped specifically for this very event, since I didn't have anything nice enough in my closet for the occasion.

My nude heels landed on the sidewalk as Garrett pulled me up and out of the car, as if I was feather light. The valet slid in the driver's seat. "Thanks, man," Garrett called to him, folding me into one of his humongous arms. He pushed my door shut and we entered the restaurant. "Hello, welcome to The

Olde Pink House," the young hostess greeted brightly.

"Thank you. We have reservations under the name Simmons," Garrett smiled politely. I noticed how his voice always had that pleasant cadence to it. So pleasant that it caused to hostess to blush slightly. "Yes of course, Mr. and Mrs. Simmons, we have you here. Elijah, can you lead Mr. and Mrs. Simmons to their table?"

A shock ran through me at the hostess' assumption and I felt my face burn.

Garrett only smiled wider, thoroughly entertained. "After you, *Mrs. Simmons*," he gestured with a grin.

My mouth fell open, before I turned and followed Elijah. Elijah turned. "Is this your first time with us?" he asked cheerfully.

"Yes," I answered.

"Oh, you're going to *love* it, Mrs. Simmons. You're going to want to come back often," he nodded assuredly with a smile.

I heard Garrett's deep chuckle behind me and fought the urge to turn around and glare at him.

We reached our table and Elijah pulled out my chair for me. I sat in it promptly and he pushed it back in. Garrett sat across from me. The table was small and lavishly decorated with twinkling crystal and silver.

"Enjoy your meal," Elijah said in closure.

"Thank you," we both said at the same time.

It was silent a moment as I took in the atmosphere of the restaurant. The lighting was warm and romantic and chandeliers glittered overhead. When my eyes found Garrett's again, I found myself taking in a whole new sight. He'd wore a black suit tonight and his large frame appeared even more foreboding in it. I'd never seen Garrett in a suit, it was certainly something I could get used to. The collar of the white undershirt he was wearing underneath his jacket was open, absent of a tie. I was granted the opportunity to peek at manly chest hair. His slanted eyes were wide and serious, and it made my stomach flip. In this lighting it was hard to tell they even *were* green. Whatever was causing his eyes to look like that was making me even more nervous. *Was he thinking the same thing that I was?* Was this finally *the* night? The night that twelve long years of buried feelings were going to be released? I had to break the stifling silence.

"It's really nice here, thank you for bringing me here," I fiddled with the napkin on my lap.

"Of course, you're welcome. I've always wanted to come here myself," he admitted. "And the night's only begun," he reminded me kindly, with a devilish twinkle in his eye.

That twinkle was all the confirmation I needed for my former suspicions.

"Yes, well..." I whispered breathily.

I was grateful for the interruption of the waitress.

"Hello, my name is Veronica. What can I start you two off with to drink? Some red wine perhaps? Or Chardonnay?" Her scarlet red hair was tied back neatly and she smiled at us with lipstick in the matching shade.

"Chardonnay would be lovely," Garrett answered.

"Okay, two Chardonnay's then?" She looked to me.

I bobbed my head, quickly agreeing. I still hadn't found my voice yet.

"Okay, any appetizers?"

I looked to Garrett and he smiled a little. "How about the blackened oysters on a half shell?"

Veronica smiled politely. "Of course, I'll go get those started for you. Anything else?" She checked.

"No, that'll be all for now. Thank you," Garrett said in his silky smooth, oh-so-charming voice, meeting her eyes.

"You're welcome," she blushed. She looked flustered as she left our table.

I laughed a little, and Garrett's eyes snapped to mine. "What's so funny?" He asked.

"*You* are," I admitted. "Are you trying to seduce the waitress?" I teased.

Garrett looked dumbfounded. "I'm not following," he furrowed his brows.

I shook my head, laughing. "Nothing, nevermind."

"Did I *sound* seductive?" He questioned, amusement slowly lighting his features.

"Forget it," I shook my head. "So, oysters, huh?" I changed the subject lamely.

"They *are* supposed to be an aphrodisiac, aren't they?" He teased, his eyes gleaming.

I raised my eyebrows at his audacity. "So I've heard," I admitted.

Like I would need more of an aphrodisiac than the man seated in front of me.

Veronica returned with our drinks and oysters. We clinked glasses and then oyster shells for good measure. We ordered our meals and talked while waiting for them.

Garrett cleared his throat awkwardly. "You, uh— you look really breathtaking in that dress tonight, Corinne," he said huskily.

I watched him with caution. "That's just the Chardonnay talking," I shrugged it off. But inside I was melting with pleasure.

"No, I *mean* it, really. That color looks so alluring on your...skin," he said, trailing off as his eyes traced my bare arms.

I had to clear my throat this time. "Well, thank you. You look really, um, handsome as well. You really fill out that suit." As soon as the words were out of my mouth, I regretted them.

His eyebrows shot up, delightedly surprised. "Oh, you think so?" The left corner of his mouth tugged up into a smirk. *Damn that smirk.* "I do try to keep up with you. I wouldn't want to embarrass you, being seen next to the likes of me," he winked.

* * *

I ordered the almond encrusted tilapia and he ordered the pecan crusted chicken breast. Our conversation flowed easily as we both reminisced on our fond childhood memories and filled each other in on some of the things we'd missed from our years spent apart. By the time we sliced into our dessert, both of us were relaxed and silly with drink. We'd went through two bottles of Chardonnay and almost all reservations were thrown out the window. I ate the last bite of cake and Garrett paid the enormous tab and we were on our way. When I rose from the table, I was surprised when Garrett grabbed my hand. Even more so, when he led me away gently with his hand on the small of my back.

The valet pulled our car forward and we got in. It was an unsaid, unspoken, known fact that we were headed to *his* apartment. The radio played music, but my ears couldn't make out what kind it was. My head was swimming with desire and nerves. Garrett was just as silent, overcome by the amount of tension in the car. Faster than I'd hoped, he'd pulled up and parked. His sleek building stood before me. He opened my door for me and I swear I could *hear* our hearts collectively beating hard together. We went inside and into the elevator to the eleventh floor. The silence was deafening, as his hand in mine became slick with sweat. The doors opened and we walked out into the hall and to Garrett's apartment. I felt like I was dreaming, like this wasn't even *real*. My feet felt like they floated here.

But this wasn't a dream, this *was* real. Garrett unlocked the door and held it open for me. I stepped inside knowing everything was about to change. I knew for a fact *I'd* never be the same. This was one of those moments, the kind people waited for their whole life. And I had waited what *felt* like for my whole life and it was happening *now,* to *me.*

Garrett shut the apartment door behind him and locked it. He turned to me, smirking. "What?" He asked.

I shook my head, stupidly grinning.

"Why are you smiling like that?" He stepped towards me, pulling me into his arms.

I sighed. "Nothing, I'm just happy," I admitted.

His eyes sparkled. "I'm happy, too."

CHAPTER TWENTY-THREE
Annette, who?

Roberta and I had both obtained the proper paperwork and licensing to open our business. We picked a quaint little brick building in downtown Savannah. It used to be an old bakery, years ago. The scent of sweetness still clung its the walls. We knew it was perfect for our little coffee shop/vintage boutique. We'd been working together and living together since we'd finished school and everything was *perfect*, a slice of heaven. *Except* my love life, that is. *That* was going nowhere. Phil and I had fizzled out a while back and I'd been single ever since.

I was working by myself one morning, when Roberta had a modeling shoot. When the bell on the door jingled. I looked up from the register to see who had entered. The blinding sun flashed, bathing the figure in bright yellow light. I winced in pain, shriveling down in my stool.

"Welcome to Vintage Only," I nearly whimpered.

"Yes, welcome it is," a familiar voice bellowed.

I gasped. "*Garrett?*"

"Who's this 'Garrett' you speak of? He sounds like an ox of a man." The sun moved to outline his shoulders and I could now make out his cheeky grin.

I tried to control my expression of pure joy that was threatening to leak through every crevice of my entirety. My face hurt from trying to contain my elated smile. "Oh I don't know, he's okay," I shrugged. "He's kind of a flake," I said, with a pucker-lipped, off-kilter, kind of a smile.

He held his heart, pretending to be wounded. "*Ouch*—that really *does* hurt," he paused before meeting me at the counter.

"So, how've you been, Corinne?" He flashed me a wide grin, leaning his massive arms across the counter. I briefly worried that the glass counter might crack.

A warm flush spread from my neck to the top of my head. "I've been well. To what do I owe this honor?" I joked. "Really, why didn't you *tell* us you were in town?" Hurt was evident in my voice.

"I wanted to surprise you," he admitted, standing up straight to his full height and using that tone in his voice that liquefied my insides to mush.

"Well, mission accomplished," I blushed, hiding my eyes from his for a moment.

Something about his gaze was so always so unintentionally intimate. I always felt as if he could see right through me.

"Actually, I'm staying *here* now…"

My eyes shot back up. "*Really?* You're moving *back?*" I gasped, delirious with pleasure.

He nodded. "Just finished moving into my new apartment."

"I also have something else I have to tell you," he cleared his throat. The way his voice deepened alarmed me.

He had a strange look on his face and it was slightly apologetic.

"Roberta knew you were coming?" I guessed stupidly. The feeling of impending nausea was hovering over me.

He shook his head quickly, and he scratched the back of his neck shamefully. "No, she has no idea I'm here either," he admitted, guiltily. Suddenly, he wouldn't meet my eye. His eyes scanned the shelves behind me. My heart dropped and felt like it landed in my stomach.

"Then what did you want to tell me?" I edged.

He shuffled on his feet nervously, simultaneously shifting his gaze from me to the shelves.

"*Garrett? Is it safe to come in now?*" A female voice teased.

All of the previous joy I felt, withered away, and was replaced by black, cold, hard glass. That seemed to crystallize and spread inside of me, freezing me on the inside.

Garrett stiffened, before forcing an impression of ease into his voice. "*Of course!* Come, come here!" His voice was the epitome of calm, but I saw the flash of discomfort in his eyes.

My nemesis walked forward with her stupid long legs and Barbie blonde hair. She walked up right behind Garrett, sliding her hand onto his left shoulder lovingly.

"Good, because I was getting tired of waiting in the car," she winked at me. Her skin was perfect, without a freckle or a blemish in sight, her baby blue eyes were the kind that men got lost in. Her wide grin exposed perfect teeth. She wore a flowing white top and her skin was perfectly sun-kissed bronze. Everything *about* her screamed 'Floridian.'

Garrett forced a strained chuckle. "Sorry about that. Corinne, this is Annette, my fiancée," he turned toward her.

My jaw dropped to the floor. I think it took me a full minute to recover.

Annette stuck her tan, bony hand in my face. "Nice you meet you, Karen," she smiled.

"Corinne. It's Corinne." I found my voice.

"Oh! I'm so *sorry*, Corinne!" She giggled. Then added flagrantly, "Garrett talks about you *all* the time."

And you still couldn't get my name right?

He blushed beside her. "We've been friends since we were kids," he interjected as his defense.

Sore subject, am I?

"That's so *sweet*, baby," she pulled him in for a deep kiss, right in front of me.

I felt my body go rigid and looked away out of politeness. Or maybe it was so I wouldn't *kill* her? I couldn't be sure.

When she pulled away, I looked up.

"*Sorry*, I just can't *help* myself. We're *so* in love," she smiled with glee. "You understand, right?"

Loving Garrett? Of course.

"Oh—no, I haven't ever...I mean, I'm not really looking for that...right now. What with running our business and all," I blushed, humiliated. For some reason Garrett was hanging onto my every word.

All I could think is, *'loser! You look like a single, love-less loser! You are going to die a crazy cat lady!'*

She gasped and reached out to touch my arm sympathetically, and I couldn't stop the way I flinched. She didn't seem to notice. "There's *always* time for *love!*" She insisted. "You know I used to be *just* like you. I was one hundred percent focused on modeling!"

I fought to not roll my eyes. A fucking *model?!?* Of course! *Typical Garrett!*

"And then I met *Garrett* and, well, *everything* changed," she turned and gazed at him, doe-eyed.

The way he smiled back at her, made me want to disintegrate into ashes to escape this agony.

"Well, I'm...I'm *happy* for you two," I lied through my teeth.

Garrett nodded. "Thank you, Corinne. What do you think *Roberta* will say?" He leaned forward, conspiring.

Just as I open my mouth to answer, the bell on the door jingled again. "Hey, batch! Who's the hottie?" Roberta swaggered in in a long flowing dress and heels. She looked fresh, like she just came from the salon rather than a grueling four hour shoot.

I guess it was a model thing. No matter what they've been doing before, they still walk into the room like a fresh breeze.

Garrett turned, along with his now fuming model fiancée.

Roberta's jaw dropped as her eyes took in the impressive man our friend had transformed into.

"Well aren't *you* a sight for sore eyes! Get over here, stud muffin! How've you been?" She grinned from ear to ear.

I know and *Garrett* knows that Roberta's not actually *attracted* to him, it's just how she talks to people. But *Annette* didn't know, and judging by the way her face turned redder and redder by the moment, she had most definitely taken it the *wrong* way. *I didn't know a tan person could turn so red...*

Roberta strode over to a blushing Garrett, and without even taking his astonished companion into account, pulls him into a gigantic hug.

"*Excuse me?*" Croaked Annette.

Roberta pulled back to glance at her, just noticing her for the first time. "Oh, *hello!* Have you been helped?"

And just like that, Roberta knocked Annette back down to size. I suddenly saw Annette in Roberta's eyes. A *stranger* standing beside *our* best friend.

CHAPTER TWENTY-FOUR

Run The Bases

"Would you like to watch a film with me?" Garrett cleared his throat awkwardly. He was nervous and it was so cute.

"Sure," I smiled politely. My heart was hammering in my chest at the mere thought of sharing a *couch* alone with him.

It wasn't the first time I'd been to his apartment, but it was the first time we'd been here 'together'. I'd always admired how he decorated it with all his interests, as opposed to it being a normal, bland bachelor pad.

I bet girls really stripped it down quick in here after seeing how interesting Garrett really was, I thought to myself. But then I dashed the thought away as soon as my stomach dipped in discomfort at the images playing in my mind.

Garrett *was* different. He had other interests besides sports, chicks and beer. He was interested in traveling, culture, history, and books. I mean, what's sexier than a man who reads? *Nothing. The answer is nothing.*

We sat down. "What would you like to see?" He turned to me.

"Surprise me," I shrugged, closing my eyes.

I heard him laugh. "Okay. But don't be upset if I get it wrong," he warned.

"You could *never* get it wrong," I admitted, I smiled, squeezing my eyes shut.

He chose a movie and I waited until I felt the couch dip beside me, before I opened my eyes again. The screen lit up and my lips turned upwards. "*Suicide Squad?*" I teased.

"You *told* me to pick!" He blushed.

"I'm just teasing you," I laughed. "You know I love this movie."

"Good," he sighed with relief. "Me too." He smiled a little, then reached over in the most natural way and slid my hand in his. The warm roughness of his skin caused a thrill to run through me. Despite the jolt within me, he didn't seem to notice.

About thirty minutes into the movie and after a lot of flirting and playful banter, Garrett's hand slid onto my thigh. My eyes fell to his hand, then slid up to his. His wide green eyes watched me with caution, his mouth turned downward in uncertainty. I smiled at him in an encouraging way. Then I looked back to the screen, unsure of what to do next. Garrett's hand began to intermittently squeeze my thigh gently. My heart was racing and my eyes had already begun to glaze over unseeingly into the screen, when Garrett scooted closer to me and put his arm around me, drawing me close. I didn't realize I'd been holding my breath, until he looked down at me and winked. I smiled and released the breath.

I could hardly concentrate on the movie while Garrett's strong arm weighed heavily upon my shoulders. His hard body was pressed against mine and his cologne was making my thoughts fuzzy. He laughed at the movie and I could feel the deep rumble reverberate inside of me. I flinched and Garrett looked down at me.

"You *okay?*" His palm squeezed my arm briefly.

I nodded. "Yeah, of course." I forced a smile at him and he looked like he knew better.

He nodded and looked at the TV. Then he paused, before turning back to me. "You know, Corinne, there's no pressure tonight. Nothing has to happen. We can take things as slow as you'd like," he spoke in a deep, cautious voice. He was looking at me like he was afraid I was going to bolt. "I can take you home whenever you want," he reminded me.

I stared at him, loving him even more in that moment. "No...I want to *stay*," I shook my head slowly.

His chest fell with relief. "Good. I want you to stay too," he smiled brightly, banishing my nerves for a second.

He lifted his left hand to my chin and held it delicately. Then with eyes on my lips, leaned down to kiss me. The kiss was soft and timid, and I think it was meant to be brief, but it turned out to be scaldingly hot. The moment his lips touched mine, my body responded. It sang with awareness, tingling and heating with electricity. He held my chin as the kiss deepened, his hand sliding to clasp my neck. One kiss melded to the next and before I knew it, Garrett was climbing over me. Our kisses broke apart as I felt his body hover over mine for an instant. He leaned back for better access to my body, before settling himself between my legs. I had barely a second to realize, 'oh, shit, this is happening.' But I didn't feel an increment of hesitation within me. My body wanted this, *I* wanted this. My dress bunched up in the process, as he knelt before me. Seeing him literally on his knees for me was something I'd always fantasized about, making me want to pinch myself, convinced I was dreaming.

We both panted, staring at each other and he chuckled a little, in surprise I think, before his eyes changed again. Green intensity bored into me. "Is *this* okay?" His hard hips dug into the middle of my inner thighs, spreading my legs further apart. His hands gripped the sensitive skin on the tops of my thighs, sliding up, higher and higher. My mouth fell open a little.

"*Uh-huh*," I breathed.

He smirked, pleased by my reactions, his dimples deepening, before the feel of my skin under his *own* hands affected him as well. He stared down at his hands on my thighs and gulped. "And *this?*" He asked, ruggedly, barely holding onto control.

He pulled me down suddenly, dragging my body down to meet with his rock hard desire. A gasp escaped me and my body sagged against the couch. "Y-*yes...*" I quivered.

His eyes had changed yet again and now looked to be more animal than man. "Are you sure?" He asked in a velvety, low voice. It was a question, a threat and a warning, all in one.

Who was this man? This was *not* the Garrett I'd known my whole life. *This* man was a sexual caveman ready to drag me into the bedroom and have his way with me. *And I fucking loved it.* I loved this new undiscovered territory I was heading into.

"Yes," I whispered, breathlessly.

His hands slid up even further then, dragging the material of my dress up with them. I gasped as I watched his eyes take in the black lace panties I was wearing. I was exposed, but suddenly that became the *second* most important thing happening. The first was the look on Garrett's face. His mouth fell slack with hunger and desire, it was written plain as day on his features. He licked his lips and brought both of his hands back down. He pushed both of his thumbs against my most sensitive spot, gently, then rubbed in slow circles.

A muffled moan escaped and his eyes shot to mine. He watched me as he did it again. I writhed from the carnal pleasure of it all. He looked on in wonder, amazed at what was happening. Suddenly he dropped down lower and I felt his fingers pull my panties to the side.

"Is this okay?" I heard him ask. But I could only see the top of his head.

My heartbeat was the loudest sound in the room as I answered, "yes."

His mouth met with me instantly and I cried out. I heard him moan as he tasted me and my hands found their way into his hair. He licked and kissed me like I was made of honey. I'd lost all awareness and was trying my hardest to hold onto control. My discretion was long gone and I was cursing and moaning repeatedly. "*Garrett, Garrett...*" I moaned his name, not even sure of what I wanted. But he knew.

He stopped and left me throbbing with pleasure. He slid my panties back over and wiped off his mouth with the back of his hand. If I thought he appeared animalistic before, now a crazed man sat before me. "I knew you'd taste like that," he mused. "Sweet and addictive, so addictive..." His eyes worshipped my body.

My body was thrumming with pleasure.

He looked focused as he gently lifted me up into a sitting position. He pressed his forehead against mine as his arms wrapped around me from behind and his hands found the zipper of my dress. He pulled it down and when his rough hands met with the smooth skin of my back, I flinched and shivered. He smiled like a boy unwrapping a present on his birthday, as he pulled down the shiny fabric from my shoulders. The dress pooled at my waist, leaving me in my matching black lace bra. He kissed me then and kept kissing down, down to my neck, my collarbone and finally my shoulder. He pulled my bra strap aside and kissed the bare skin there. Then his hands met behind me again, as he reached back and unclasped the bra, sliding it down my arms. It landed on top of my dress. Garrett leaned back to look at me. "Corinne, you were *so* worth the wait. You are so *beautiful*," he breathed.

Before I could respond, he leaned down and buried his head between my breasts. He wasted no time, drawing a nipple into his mouth and sucking it. He did the same to the other, nibbling them for good measure. My moans had gotten out of hand again, when he scooped me into his arms.

"I think it's time we take this party in the bedroom, don't you?" He winked.

He carried me in his strong arms like I was a doll, towards his bedroom. The song "Sucker For Pain" played in the background as we entered the dark hall that led to Garrett's bedroom.

CHAPTER TWENTY-FIVE
By The Moonlight

Oh God, *this was really happening*. Garrett laid me down on his bed gently and I propped myself up onto my elbows in anticipation. It'd been years since I had sex, but I had the feeling this would be *nothing* like the other times. It was dark and his comforter was cool under my skin. The only light was moonlight filtered in through a window curtain that was slightly open. I could only make out his glowing silhouette. It oddly made him look like he was under a pale blue spotlight, performing just for me. He slid off his suit jacket, letting it fall carelessly to the floor. He nearly ripped off his shirt and I was gifted with the vision of his muscled torso and his hairy chest basked in the moonlight. He licked his lips while staring down at me the way a starved man looks at his last meal. We didn't speak. We didn't have to. His eyes said it all. *The things I'm going to do to you*, was what I was reading from them now. I watched in shock as he made quick work of unbuttoning his pants and pulling them down. He sprung out, thick and mighty, straining against his boxers. They barely contained the packaged treasure within. I could already see a peek of pale skin and hair from the opening that was barely held by one lone button.

He reached down, pulling me down by my hips. My breath exhaled sharply through my lips as I fell onto my back.

"*Garrett...*" I chuckled anxiously.

"*Corinne,*" he growled in response, his dimples deepening in the shadows.

His hands loosened their grip on my hips and hooked into the material of my dress that was bunched at my hips, taking my bra along with it. He pulled them down firmly and I lifted my body slightly to assist. He shimmied them down my thighs and my legs tantalizingly slowly, skimming the fabric and his fingers across my skin, eliciting more shivers from me. He tossed it aside.

For a full minute he just stared at me. Then he commanded. "Touch yourself."

I gasped. "*What?*"

Had I heard him correctly?

"You *heard* me. *Touch* yourself. I. Want. To. Watch. You," he annunciated each word.

My mouth fell open, and for a moment I considered refusing. But Garrett's eyes were so wanton that I couldn't deny his request.

I felt my right hand twitch before complying. My hand slid to my chest first. Garrett watched, entranced. My hand fell to the dip between my breasts. I traced around them with my fingers before grabbing them one at a time gently, toying with my nipples. My breathing was uneven under Garrett's intense gaze.

Garrett's mouth fell slack. "*Lower*," he groaned, like he was in pain. "Touch your pussy," he purred seductively, begging.

The hypnotic look in Garrett's eyes gave me the bravery I needed. Desire pooled naked in his eyes as he watched my hand skim lower and lower, until it was underneath my thong panties. Garrett's hands twitched at his sides. He wanted to touch me so badly. My fingers met with delicate skin and wetness and I squirmed, trying to relax.

"Don't be shy..." he coaxed. Then he ran his hand down his hard length just once.

Oh? Is this what was going to happen?

He saw me watching and unbuttoned that one. Small. Button.

He smiled as his impressive member sprung out. It was so engorged, and throbbing, and *big*. I couldn't help but stare at it, wide-mouthed and stunned.

"That's right, baby," he cajoled. "You can watch *me*, too." He grabbed himself with his right hand and stroked down. Then he waited. "Do continue," he encouraged me.

His words rang in my ears, especially the part when he called me *baby*.

I realized I had stopped participating and rubbed myself with renewed fervor. He joined in, stroking himself with his mouth hanging open, his eyes were sex-crazed and blazing with want. I was surprised how turned on I was, I never imagined being okay with this sort of thing.

A moan slipped out and my breaths quickened as my hand rubbed faster and the wetness spread to all of my fingers. I watched as Garrett became unhinged. He let go of himself. "*Stop.*"

My hand stilled and he pulled down his boxers decidedly. Then I was able to see the full monty. I slipped up my hand, resting it on my stomach. Garrett slowly lowered to his knees, watching me. He leaned forward and gingerly picked up my hand.

I watched in disbelief. *He's not going to...*

He opened his mouth and sucked my fingers and my whole body jolted to life all over again.

I stood corrected.

His eyes were predatory and I shivered from the strong pull they had on me. He released my quivering hand, and his hands ran down to my panty line. I heard a rip and flinched. A second later Garrett held what was left of my panties in front of my face.

"Garrett, what the—" I gasped.

He smirked proudly. "I'll buy you new ones," he reassured me. "Still want to do this?" He dared, a mischievous glint in his eye.

"More than ever," I breathed.

"Do you trust me?" He asked, a flash of the old Garrett shining through for a second.

That question caught me off guard. "Y—yes. Of course I do, Garrett," I stammered.

"Good," he beamed. Then he stood and leaned over me, picking up both of my hands. I watched him with confusion as he used my panties to tie my wrists together.

"Holy shit," I breathed. "Do I need a safe word or something?" I asked, with incredulity.

He chuckled, then dropped his hands to my ass, groping it and lifting me slightly. He slid me further up on the bed. Then he lifted my arms above my head, grabbing both of my wrists in his right hand, and pinning them against the bed. He held them there firmly, kissing me softly at the corner of my mouth and my jawline. I was melting inside already and we hadn't even begun.

"Spread 'em, Powell," he teased, reaching down to push my thighs further apart with his left hand. I gasped and met his eyes.

"Who *are* you?" I accused.

He laughed. "You *know* who I am!"

"Not *this* side of you..." I admitted.

He answered with a frisky smile. He suddenly sat back onto his heels, crawling over to his nightstand. He opened the drawer and quickly retrieved a condom. Then he sat back on his heels once more, admiring me. I fidgeted under his intense gaze, as he opened the condom and rolled it onto himself while staring at me.

"You look like a dream, Corinne," he said huskily. "I mean, this is something I'd dream about," he clarified. "I'm not dreaming, am I?"

A giggle erupted out of my chest. "No, you're not dreaming. Come here, I'll prove it," I lifted my right foot and pointed the toes, barely poking him in the chest.

He growled and caught my foot, biting down on my big toe.

"*Ow!*" I protested, attempting to pull to yank back my leg. But he was faster and stronger than me and he pinned it down by grabbing my thigh. I gasped. He hovered over me again like a steel cage. He caught my bottom lip in his teeth and bit down gently and I whimpered. When he released it, his green eyes were primal. "I want you so bad, Corinne. Say I can have you?" He purred.

"You already know you can," I panted.

He closed his eyes, relishing in my permission. I felt him reach down and push himself against me. Two beats later, he pushed himself inside of me.

He groaned deeply and shut his eyes. *My* eyes however, flew open at invasive feeling. He was much too large and I wasn't sure I could handle him anymore. "*Ah!*" I cried out, instinctively drawing my knees upward.

He kissed me gently on the lips, soothing me. "It's okay, Corinne," he murmured lovingly, tracing the contours of my cheek. "We'll start slow," he reassured me. I didn't miss the promise in his eyes that said, *'but we won't stay that way.'*

,

CHAPTER TWENTY-SIX

Taste

"Don't look at me like that," Garrett said while sipping his coffee. His eyes peeked over the mug.

We were having breakfast in his small breakfast nook. The kitchen was white, as were the walls, table and chairs. The sunlight filtering in through the white curtained window was so bright, making it appear like we borrowed a room from heaven. Dust motes swirled around in the air in dreamlike way. I was reveling at the soreness between my legs. Every movement reminded me of what had occurred last night. *What a pleasant way to be hurting*, I thought.

"Like what?"

"Like I'm going lay you across the table at any moment," he lowered the mug, snickering.

"Aren't you?" I tested.

He only shook his head with a smile.

"You know what I'm waiting for." I crossed my arms.

"I *do?*" His eyebrow quirked up.

"Yes."

He stared, puzzled. "Help me out here?"

"An explanation," I offered.

"*For?*"

"For pulling the rug out from under me last night, Garrett! A *warning* would've been nice!"

"A *warning?*" He furrowed his eyebrows, but a smile played at the corners of his lips.

I hugged myself and flushed. "Are you...*always* like that?"

Realization dawned on his face, before it fell in shame. "You didn't like it?"

I laughed haughtily. "You know I *did*. I just didn't *expect* that from you," I admitted. "I mean...I've never *done* anything *like* that before."

A flush crept up his neck and he set down his mug, his face falling into his hands momentarily. "I haven't either," he said when he lifted his head. His cheeks were still pink. A shy smile tugged at his mouth.

"*Really?*" I sat up, uncrossing my arms.

He nodded. "*Really.* I don't really know what came over me last night. I've never been like that before. I'm sorry if you didn't like it. I can be different next time?" He offered.

He reached across the table, taking my hand in his. He stroked it gently. His eyes melted with sincerity.

I was already breathing unevenly. "No...I mean, I'll tell you if I don't like something. I guess I just wanted to know," I shrugged.

He nodded.

My phone buzzed on the small round table and fell off of the edge, landing on the floor. "Shit," I bent to retrieve it.

Mine and Garrett's hands broke apart, as he tried to reach for it at the same time. I beat him to it, but became distracted by the sight under the table. Garrett's pants were hugging him in the most delicious way. I paused to stare for a moment too long.

"Corinne?" I heard him call from above the table and I bumped my head on the under side of it. The table's contents clinked together. I raised my head and my cheeks were burning. *Was I busted?*

He seemed to catch onto my change in mood. "Everything go okay down there?" He checked, his eyes mocking.

I sat up and cleared my throat. "Yes. I got my phone." Then I checked it, trying to emphasize my innocence.

It was a message from Roberta.

So??? How'd last night go? I smirked at my phone. '*Oh, I'll fill you in on that later.*' I thought.

I licked my lips, recalling just how impressive Garrett's manhood had been. I realized how badly I wanted to explore that further.

Garrett arrested me with a look. "Having a thought you'd care to share?"

I giggled. "Nope."

I got up to put my dishes in the sink. I felt Garrett rise and follow behind me. I rinsed off the dishes in the sink, and I felt his arms encircle my waist. "*Tell me,*" he urged behind me.

"No way," I laughed.

"*Please?*" He pleaded.

I shook my head, drying my hands on a towel. I twirled out of his arms and danced past him. He watched me with amusement. I looked over my shoulder. "I guess you could always torture it out of me."

"Ooh challenge accepted," he threatened.

I took off running, but it was no use. Garrett was impossibly fast. He'd captured me in no time. He caught me by the hips and his left hand tangled into the back of my hair. He tugged it back, drawing my neck upward, while his right hand grabbed in between my legs. A yelp escaped me.

"*Big mistake*," he whispered into my ear, biting it gently.

He rubbed me in between my legs mercilessly. Making my legs want to collapse. "Want to tell me yet?"

"No," I panted.

He chuckled, loving this game, knowing he would win. He released me and threw me over his shoulder like a Neanderthal. The world went upside down.

"*Garrett!*"

I kicked and hit him, but my assaults were useless. He walked the short hall and threw me onto the bed. I bounced roughly. "You're *doing* it again!" I panted.

"*Am I?* I guess you bring it out in me," his mouth hung open, his eyes were bright and playful.

He grabbed me by my ankles and pulled me down. My makeshift pajamas (his t-shirt and boxers) were pushed up, exposing me on top and bottom. "Well, that's a bonus," he smirked.

I pulled at them frantically. But my eyes fell again to that gigantic bulge in his pants. Garrett's eyes followed and he cocked a brow. "Something caught your attention?"

My eyes were panicked, as I realized he already knew the answer. I sat up, determined. Garrett stood hovering at the edge of the bed, looking like he was made of stone. His face only faltered slightly, indicating he was nervous. My eyes met with his, and I hoped they were as demure as they felt. "I never got to taste you last night and I'd really like to," I confessed in a murmur.

Garrett's sharp intake of breath pleased me. I was happy I was able to shock him the way he did me.

"You never got to *taste* me?" He croaked, blinking hard. "I suppose that's true...I—*please* oblige yourself. I'm here for the taking...or the *tasting*, I guess," he chuckled self-consciously.

I smiled in response, choosing to remain silent the way he had last night. The more anticipation, the better.

I tugged on his belt, unbuckling it. Then I unbuttoned his pants, and unzipped them. He was so hard and so ready. I grabbed him hard, suddenly feeling hungry with desire. I heard him groan loudly from above. Then I pulled down his pants and boxers, pushing them down around his ankles and leaving them there. He had a glorious cock. I held it in both hands, licking the tip experimentally. His chest was rising and falling with quick breaths. He tasted good, and of course he did. I drew him into my mouth immediately and sucked. Garrett moaned loudly.

"Christ woman, you're going to be the death of me," he growled.

CHAPTER TWENTY-SEVEN
The "L" Word

That evening, back at mine and Roberta's apartment, I soaked in the tub. My mind replayed the events that took place like my own little porno movie starring me and Garrett. I reached down and gently touched myself again, in between my legs, just check that it was real. I winced when my hand met with tender skin. I was sore and there was no denying it. *Yup, it really happened.*

Just this morning, Garrett had stopped my oral assault on him and instead pulled me on top of him. I could still imagine the feel his rough hands on me, the way his fingers had dug into my hips, pushing me down onto him. The way his impenetrable eyes had worshipped my body as it moved, wasn't something I could easily forget either. I'd never had sex like *that* before, and the fact that it was with *Garrett*, couldn't make me happier.

How mortifying it would have been if we had been incompatible in bed!

It would've been a deal breaker on both ends.

A loud slam interrupted my contemplations and I strained to hear what it was. Someone was giggling and banging around loudly and it sounded like they were getting closer. The bathroom door swung open and I flinched forward, covering my chest. Luckily bubbles obscured the lower part of my body. I was just about to yell, 'Hey!', when the shower curtain was ripped aside.

I screamed at the top of my lungs as Roberta and Rodney nearly fell on top of me. They were too lip-locked and body-entangled to notice immediately, but my screams alerted them well enough.

"Oh my God, *Corinne!*" Roberta exclaimed, yanking the curtain back into place immediately, but not before I caught Rodney's jaw dropped smile.

"*I'm sorry! I'm sorry!* I didn't know you were in here!" Roberta pleaded. "We were um..."

I covered my face with my hands. The small space of bathtub now felt like a sauna and I was sweating in embarrassment. "I can *guess*, Roberta!" I yelled. "Just *go!*" I pleaded. I knew what they were about to *do*, have some good clean fun in the shower.

"I'm *so* sorry!" Roberta repeated again. "*Apologize*, Rodney!" I heard her smack him.

"Sorry, um, Corinne," I heard his booming voice mutter awkwardly.

"It's *fine*, just *go!*" I yelled, impatient for them to leave.

I didn't uncover my face until I heard them shuffle out, resuming their wild make-out session all the way down the hall. I waited until I heard Roberta's door shut, before I rose out of the tub, draining it and wrapping myself in a towel. I poked my head out and checked both ways before quickly scurrying down the hall to my room. I shut the door, taking care to *lock* it this time, and got dressed in my pajamas. Then I sat on my bed and proceeded to stare at the comforter for a full five minutes. As if replaying the devastating event in my head enough times would change the outcome. Roberta had already seen me naked, but I could've gone without such a perfect specimen as *Rodney* looking upon *my* imperfect body for the rest of my life. My phone buzzed against the comforter and it broke my misery induced trance, for that of which I was grateful for. It was getting me absolutely nowhere. It was Garrett.

Busy tonight? An irreversible smile lit my face.

Just then, I heard yelling and my smile did fade.

"Get *out!* Get the *hell* out!"

I sprang to my feet, worried for Roberta. But I realized quickly I shouldn't have. As soon as I swung the door open, I saw Roberta throwing Rodney's clothes at him.

"Baby, let me *explain!*" He begged, stumbling backwards toward the door, frightened. He was only wearing his boxers again, and I trained my eyes to look at Roberta only. As she threw his clothes, he caught them one by one. He dropped his shoes a few times, and they landed with a muted thump on the floor, before he could snatch them back up into his arms. His face was apologetic. He almost looked like he was going to cry.

"*No!* You *know* I don't play around with this stuff. Get *out!*" Roberta opened the door and pushed him out, slamming the door in his shocked, pretty face.

She locked it and turned on her heel quickly, pressing her back against the door. She was panting and her cheeks were flushed. Dark strands of her hair fell onto her face. Her wild blue eyes met mine.

I remained paused in the doorway of my room. "Are you *okay*, Roberta? What happened?"

She only stared at me, like she'd seen a ghost.

Alarmed, I took a hesitant step forward. "Are you—did he *hurt* you?"

I tried to inspect her from afar for injuries, which was easy to do, since she was wearing only hot pink undergarments. But I didn't see any marks or bruises.

She shook her head 'no' in a daze.

"Well then, what did he *do*, Roberta? You can *tell* me," I asked, in a comforting voice. I stepped closer and closer until I was standing directly in front of her.

Her eyes focused finally, her pupils fixing into sharp points. "He told me he loved me," she breathed.

Surprise ran through me. "*What?*"

"We were about to make love..." Her chin dropped and she shook her head slightly, trying to understand. "And he said it and...." her eyes widened. "I freaked out. *Oh, shit*. I *fucked up, Corinne!* I *panicked!*" Her hand flew to her mouth and her eyes widened with realization.

I bit my lip to stifle my smile. She held her arms out. "I mean, *who* says that so *soon?* We only got back together a few weeks ago! Isn't it *too soon?*

Don't you think it *is?*" She desperately sought out my opinion.

I shrugged. "You guys have a history together. Don't be like me and Garrett and waste *years* now," I warned her with a short laugh.

"*Shit!* Oh my *God!* What did I *do? Why* did I throw him out?" She paced around.

I tried to not smile too hard. I tried to remind myself of how *she* was feeling. And I knew *exactly* how she was feeling. She was realizing that *she* loved *him* too.

"Why did I *do* that?" She murmured to herself. She turned to me. "Do you think it's too *late?* Do you think I *ruined* it?" Her panicked gaze met with mine.

There was a knock on the door. She flew to it, unlocking it and throwing it open. It was Garrett. His eyes widened in alarm.

"*Oh, God. So sorry!* Sorry, sorry!" He covered his eyes with his hands. "I didn't mean to interrupt," he opened his fingers to peek at me. I waved at him awkwardly. "...Whatever was going on *here*...?" He finished, confused.

Rodney suddenly appeared behind Garrett, looking like a frightened child. "*Rodney!*" Roberta yelled, in relief.

He stepped around Garrett cautiously. "*Roberta?*" His eyes were filled with tears.

She ran to him and jumped in his arms. "Oh, I'm so *sorry!* I *love* you! I *do!* I love you *too!*" She wrapped her arms around his neck, kissing him. He kissed her back and she wrapped her legs around him. He carried her into the house and they landed on the couch. They continued to kiss, grope and make sexual sounds while me and Garrett stood awkwardly in the midst of it.

Garrett shook his head and met my gaze. "Want to get out of here?"

"Yes."

CHAPTER TWENTY-EIGHT
Showtime

"Give me five minutes," I held up a finger to Garrett. He nodded.

I jogged past Roberta and Rodney, who barely noticed me, and back into my room. I changed into my favorite jeans and a tank top. Slipping on my sandals, I made the quick decision to leave with my hair wet.

"Are they *always* like that?" Garrett gave me a sidelong glance, as we walked down the hall, hand in hand.

"No, this is pretty new actually," I admitted. "But I have seen him half naked and today he saw me *naked, naked*," I added, thoughtfully.

Garrett stopped walking and I felt my hand pull against his. I turned around and his expression was disbelief mixed with vexation. He arched a brow. "You're *kidding* me, right?"

I turned to face him. "I wish I *was!* It was *humiliating!* I was in the *bath!*" I explained, scoffing.

His face transformed into a more composed expression. "Oh. It sounds like it. Was *Roberta* there?" He attempted to broach the subject slyly.

I then had to explain to him what had happened, from the humiliating incident, up to the bizarre fight between Roberta and Rodney. When he was satisfied, he started to walk again.

"So where to?" I asked, once we walked outside. It was humid and cloudy and raining again. The sky was a dull blue color. "No *outdoor* activities?" I smiled in question. The rain dampened my already wet hair and misted into my eyes. Rain droplets collected in my lashes, making my vision temporarily blurry.

I watched Garrett's blurry face respond, by laughing, "not unless you want to get soaked."

We climbed into his car and I shivered. He turned up the heat automatically. "Thanks," I muttered and he smiled.

He pulled out into the street and began to drive. "I thought maybe we could go to see a movie, what do you think?" He turned to me.

"Ooh, yes! I'd *love* that!" I bounced in my seat.

He grinned at me and grabbed my hand. It was so warm and enveloped mine in the most pleasant way.

We chatted briefly while driving. When we arrived, we bought our tickets to The Rock's newest action flick. We bought snacks and took our seats. Garrett had brought in a warm parka that'd he'd found in his car and had draped it affectionately over my shoulders. It was heavy and warm and about three sizes too big for me, which made it all the more cozy. About halfway through the movie, I had to use the restroom. I whispered to Garrett and handed him his jacket.

When I was finished in the bathroom, I stopped to glance at my reflection and felt horror run through me. My hair was a crazy, curly, frizzy disaster. It stood about two inches taller than usual. I couldn't believe that I was walking around in such a love stricken haze that I didn't properly consider what the humidity and rain would do to my natural curls!

"*Shit!*" I rushed to the mirror and attempted to smooth down my hair, but it was no use. My curls only sprang right back up, lively and wild as ever. I didn't even have a hair tie on me to rectify the situation. I laughed at my pink cheeked, fluffy-haired reflection, realizing I didn't care.

Love seemed to dull all other senses and all other cares in the world. I shrugged and skipped out of the bathroom. On my way back, my phone buzzed and I pulled it out to check it.

Corinne, I am so sorry about earlier. I didn't mean to kick you out of the house! We just lost control for a while there. You understand, right?

I smiled and leaned against the wall, texting Roberta my reply. *You didn't kick me out. I left, remember? And of course I understand. Just, um, remember to knock next time, okay?*

Okay! ;) Sorry! Where'd you go anyway?

We're at the movies.

Aw, now I wish we had came too! We need to double date now that we both have boyfriends!

A wave of discomfort ran through me. *Woah, slow down, pony. Me and Garrett haven't put a title on what's going on here between us! But I'm happy for you! And yes, that does sound fun!*

Mm-hmm I know exactly what is going on between you two and so do you! Deny it all you want!

I giggled to myself, then decided I'd better get back to my date.

I gotta go. Have fun and stay out of my room! I joked.

Haha! You too! Are you coming home tonight?

I thought for a minute. *I don't know.* I answered honestly.

See you tomorrow! She texted me. Damn, she knew me well.

I realized I'd spent much too long in the hall and rushed back to my seat. Garrett smiled with relief when he saw me. Taking a deep breath, he said, "oh good, you're back. I was starting to think you ran out on me," he admitted, in breathy chuckle.

"You think I'd run out on *you?*" I smiled adoringly at him.

"I *hoped* you wouldn't," he chuckled quietly, sliding his heavy arm over me and hugging me close.

"I'd have to be dragged away now," I raised my eyebrows at him, smirking.

His face lit with pleasure in the dark theatre. "*Really?*" He leaned in and whispered. "That good, *am I?*" He teased.

I shivered, thinking sensual thoughts. I closed my eyes briefly, relishing in the sound of his voice.

"Now, don't go getting a big head about it," I answered breathily.

"*Me?* Never," he smirked.

I bit my lip and stared at him, wondering if we *were* going back to his place after this. I certainly *wanted* to.

He grinned, amused. "Don't you want to watch the movie?"

I shook my head. "You're more entertaining."

He looked skeptical. "More entertaining than *The Rock?*"

"You *are* my rock," I purred.

He shook his head with a smile and turned back to the screen. I reluctantly did the same. But I couldn't concentrate on it. My imagination was running wild. Garrett scooted in his seat beside me and I wondered if he was having the same problem. I was trying hard to hold back my smile.

A naughty idea formed in my mind and I pulled Garrett's hand onto my lap. I could see him from my peripheral vision and noticed him twitch. I waited a moment, before picking his hand back up and using his dangling fingers to skim across my thighs. I peeked at him and his mouth was hanging open slightly. His chest rose and fell slowly. I brought his hand higher until his fingers dangled in between my legs, hearing his breath hitch beside me. I smiled a tiny satisfied smile, before dropping his hand and pressing it against me. He jerked forward, covering up his shock with a fake cough.

He snatched his hand back, chuckling quietly. "*Okay*, you win," he whispered, his eyes smoldering in the dark.

"I *do?*" I played stupid.

He stood and held out his hand to me.

"Where are we going?" I whispered, looking around in the near empty theater. I put my hand in his.

"You *know* where," he threatened.

CHAPTER TWENTY-NINE
Run Away Baby

"You're insatiable," Garrett murmured, as he gazed at me adoringly. "Woman, what am I going to do with you?" He teased.

I chuckled lazily, lying partially wrapped in his thick arms, and partially wrapped in his silky sheets. "You ran out of ideas already?" I joked.

"Hmmm, no. I've got plenty of those," he grinned. He raised his right hand, his left was still wrapped around my waist as I propped my chin up on his broad chest. He ran his fingers through my soft curls. "I love your hair when it's natural," he commented, absentmindedly.

A warm flush spread across my cheeks and I dipped my head down to hide my face. "Shy, are we?" His voice warmed like melted brown sugar.

I sighed. "I have to work early in the morning. Can you take me home?" I lifted my head to gaze at him.

He seemed almost hurt at first, but quickly trained his face to appear indifferently polite. I immediately regretted being so brusque with him.

"You can stay here?" He offered. "I wouldn't have a problem taking you in the morning?"

"I'm sure you *wouldn't,*" I snorted.

He made a castigating face. "You know what I meant."

I smiled.

Rain continued to fall in sheets outside, making the idea of staying the night here all the more appealing. I thought about how I didn't have any of my things and how I'd be interfering with Garrett's morning routine though.

"Thank you, but I really need to go home tonight. No matter how appealing you make it sound to stay." I scooted up on his body and pressed my lips against his softly. My body tingled from the feel of his lips against mine and I tried to ignore it. "Thanks for the date," I smiled at him when we broke apart.

"Guess we'll never know what happened at the end of the movie," he pretended to express lament over it.

"That's easy, The Rock saves the day."

"Oh, really? How can you be so sure?" He tested.

"The Rock always saves the day," I laughed.

* * *

Garrett drove me home and I entered the apartment with caution. *Who would've ever thought a random naked man roaming their apartment would be something they had to worry about?* But when I entered, the apartment was dark and quiet. *Good*, I thought. *They're done for the evening.* I tip-toed through the dark and successfully made it to my room without running into a wall, tripping, or stubbing my toe. I changed back into my pajamas, lit a relaxing candle and nestled into my bed. Louise pushed open my door and hopped on with me.

"Weezy! Come here, girl!" She approached me slowly, inquisitively. She neared and sniffed at my hand suspiciously.

I smiled. "You know where I've been, don't you? There's no hiding *anything* from you, is there?"

She seemed to accept the scent of Garrett, as well known friend, giving in and curling into my lap.

"Yes, you *know* him. Yes, I've been with *Garrett*," I cooed to her, petting her soft fur. "Do you like him *too*, Weezy?" I continued. She looked right up at me, staring into my eyes as if she understood. "Rowww," she meowed loudly.

I laughed. "I like him too...*way* too much," I sighed.

I laid down on my side, scooting her with me. Her purring lulled me to sleep within minutes. When I woke, the candle I'd lit had burned out and the whole room was dark. Rain still pattered outside and a dim gray light shone in through the window, indicating the early hour of the morning. I had the sense that I wasn't alone in the room, so I looked around me, abruptly alarmed by the shadow sitting beside my bed.

"Don't freak ou—" The voice warned, but it was too late.

I screamed as the hand reached for me. "*Shh!!* You'll wake him *up!* I'm not ready to deal with *male* in the morning!" Roberta urged.

"What the *hell*, Roberta!" I rolled over on my side, exasperated with Roberta, and irritated by my near blindness without my glasses or contacts on. "You almost gave me a *heart attack!*" I breathed, throwing the covers over my head, annoyed.

She giggled beside me. "Sorry, you were out, dude. Want to go for a run with me before work?" She beamed at me.

I threw the blankets back off. "Are...you...*crazy?*" I huffed in her general direction. I reached for my glasses and slipped them on.

I felt guilty when I saw Roberta's face, and even more guilty when she said, "we just haven't spent much time together lately," she pouted.

She looked so cute and sporty in her leggings, tank and hat.

I sighed, already smiling. "Let me get dressed."

Twenty minutes later, I was dressed and under-caffeinated for the occasion. We quietly crept through the house, careful not to wake a sleeping Rodney. We took off on foot as soon as we rounded the corner from our apartment. It was sprinkling lightly and it felt amazing. We fell into a steady pace, with Roberta in the lead.

"Come on, slow-poke!" She teased.

I pressed on, my leg muscles starting to scream in protest. "I'm *coming! We can't* all have *super-model* legs, you know!" I complained.

The drizzle of rain mixed with the sweat cooling my head and back as I panted, listening to the rhythm that our feet made against the pavement. I was suddenly glad I had came. I hadn't ran in forever and I was beginning to enjoy myself. I had a sudden burst of energy and ran harder, passing Roberta.

"*What* the??" She exclaimed as I passed her. "Get it, girl!" She called behind me.

An elated smile spread across my face even though every bone in my body was aching. I ran around a corner, leaving Roberta in the dust. When my body couldn't go anymore, I stopped running and put my hands on my knees, wheezing for air. As I waited for Roberta, my eyes caught something else. I blinked back the sweat that had dripped into my eyes to be sure that I was seeing clearly.

Garrett sat in the restaurant in front of me, I could clearly see him through the window. He was dressed in his work clothes. The one thing I couldn't reconcile, was the other female with him. I straightened up, feeling the sweat slide down my back. A pretty blonde leaned forward, and I could make out her face, it was *Annette*. She said something to Garrett and he bursted into laughter. She joined along and soon they were in fits together. The careless happiness I spotted nearly soldered my insides together. They were beaming at each other, and I was going blind and numb with fury.

Roberta ran up finally, thoroughly winded. "You're a *maniac*, Corinne!" She accused, doubling over and chuckling breathlessly.

She caught my irate stare and rigid stance. "Corinne, what are you *looking* at?" She whispered, worriedly.

She followed my gaze and her mouth fell open. "Oh, *shit*."

I marched right up to the restaurant's glass window and smacked my palm against it. Everyone in the restaurant looked up at the same time, including Garrett and Annette. As soon as he caught my eye, I flipped him the bird, and took off in a sprint back towards home.

CHAPTER THIRTY
Guilt Trip

My lungs ached and burned. Every muscle protested, but still I charged on. My vision was bleary with tears and rain. It didn't matter. *Nothing* mattered. Roberta's voice calling behind me, faded more and more. I rounded corners and ducked down alleys. I had no idea where I was going, but I knew I wasn't going home *anymore*. I had changed direction, deciding at the last minute that home would be the first place they'd go to look for me, and I didn't want to be found right now. My phone was buzzing like crazy in my pocket, but I made no move to reach for it. All too soon, I heard strong footfalls behind me.

"*Corinne!*" Garrett thundered.

Dammit, he was *fast*. As stealthy as a marathon runner, even in his work clothes. It didn't matter if I'd had a *twenty* minute head start, he'd still have caught up to me in no time. But for *once* in my life, I *didn't* want to see him. I ignored him and continued to flee.

"Corinne, *stop!*" He commanded.

I kept running, rebelling against my own body and his words. Tears fell steadily down my cheeks and I wiped at them helplessly. I was running out of steam and I didn't want to see him or talk to him, so I quickly came up with a plan. Unbeknownst to me, I had taken us right into the older part of downtown. An abandoned brick building lie ahead. It had a strange small door that touched the ground, it was open. I knew Garrett would never be able to fit in *there*, so I ran over to it and slid in quickly, scraping my palms.

Garrett's pounding feet came to a halt. "*What the?* Corinne!" He huffed, exasperated. "Come out of there," he crooned, lovingly.

I could see his strong legs and torso. His hands rested on his hips as he caught his breath. The concrete underneath me was wet and it was dark inside of the building.

"Leave me *alone*, Garrett!" I yelped, sounding like a petulant child. "*Go away!*" My voice broke.

He sighed and crouched down, attempting to peer in at me. "Don't make me come in there and get you," he threatened.

"I'd like to see you *try!*" I challenged hotly.

He chuckled angrily, but it sounded more like a growl. "Will do, my dear."

Before I could react, his hand reached in and grasped my ankle. I guess I underestimated the *length* of his arms. I turned quickly and tried to grab at something, *anything*, but there was nothing to grab. The building was empty, save for cobwebs. I flailed on my stomach, my fingers scraping against cold concrete. I felt him tug at me. Both of his hands wrapped around my ankle and I slid towards the door. I kicked at him with my free leg, but he soon had one hand clasped around that ankle too.

"Let me *go!*" I yelled, grabbing onto the edges of the door in resistance. He pried my fingers off easily and pulled me out of the hideaway. I tried to go back in and he grunted with exertion, holding me firmly by the waist.

"Sorry, my dear, I lied. I *don't* fit in there, so I *had* to pull you out," he explained.

I kicked at him again, then stood to face him, shaking with rage. He stood up as well.

"I *told* you to leave me *alone!*" I growled.

His eyes were full of sympathy, when he got a closer look at my tear stained cheeks and red-rimmed eyes.

"I'm so sorry, Corinne. I feel awful. Will you let me explain?" He pleaded.

I stared him down, assuming my burning eyes would be enough answer.

He moved to gently gather me into his arms, and I fought him like a badger. "Don't *touch* me!" I pushed him. My arms felt like tiny twigs that he could snap if he so wished. My hands pushing against his torso, may as well have been like pushing against the thick of a tree trunk. Fighting him was futile, but I still felt like I had to do it.

"Corinne..." He stepped forward. "*Please*," he implored.

"*No!* You don't *get* to talk!" I pointed a finger in his face.

I stalked off and he jogged behind me, grabbing my arm and turning me around. He tried again to hold me and, I slapped him clean across the face. He barely flinched. He was calm and focused, as he attempted to contain me by holding me in a steel tight bear hug. I pushed and slapped and even scratched, growling and grunting like a desperate animal. Garrett's face was strained as he took my assaults like a champ. I tried to loosen his hold, but to no avail. He waited patiently for me to run out of energy, which of course, eventually happened. Finally, I broke down in tears and fell weakly into his arms. He let me lean my weight against him, as he slowly sat on the ground, holding me as I sobbed. I had no more fight left in me, but unfortunately I still had plenty of tears.

"You're back *together* or what? You and Annette?" I finally whimpered.

"*No*, Corinne. We're not back together. I'm not in love with her," he said gently.

"But you *love* her?" I sniffled.

He sighed. "I will always care for her. But it'll never compare to how I feel for *you*."

I looked up at him, his expression was weary. I was starting to feel embarrassed at my amazing display of emotions.

"Why is she *here?*"

He paused a moment, careful to answer. "She was in town and wanted to get together for coffee, that's all."

"And you didn't think to ask me if I *cared* if you two got coffee?" I spat.

His eyebrows shot up at my audacity. "Honestly? I didn't think you'd care."

My face flamed and I looked away. Why *did* I care? I'd turned into some jealous mega-monster. I was wishing more and more that I could climb back into that tiny Alice In Wonderland door and never come back.

Roberta interrupted us then, pulling up in her car. When she'd had time to go and retrieve it, I'd had no idea. Had we been gone that *long?* She parked and hopped out. "Oh, *good,* you *found* her," she breathed. She was clearly still thoroughly winded from the whole ordeal. She gasped suddenly. "Is she *hurt?*" She asked, as she took in the sight of me on the floor being cradled by Garrett.

He chuckled. "No, but I wish I could say the same for *myself.*" He rose to his feet and pulled me up. I walked away from him like a child who just got let out of time out.

Roberta tried to meet my eye, but I only stalked past her and to her car. She followed me questionably and got back into her car. I opened the car door, and was about to climb in, when I heard Garrett.

"Corinne!" He called.

I looked up.

His slacks and dress shirt were rumpled and dirty. I immediately felt guilty for being responsible for his disheveled appearance. He ran a hand through his hair, ruffling it.

"My place tonight, seven o'clock. We need to talk about...*this*," he said solemnly, gesturing between us.

My mouth fell open at the graveness of his tone, but I nodded and slid into the car, shutting the door behind me.

CHAPTER THIRTY-ONE
Coward

"Okay Rinnie, tell me your game plan?" Roberta asked as she drove.

"For what?" I dropped my head into my hands, groaning.

"You know—with you and Garrett. What have you decided?"

"What do you mean?"

Roberta shot me a look. "Well, obviously you sort of freaked out on him hardcore."

"Like you did on Rodney?" I muttered, glancing at her sideways. I regretted the words immediately after I'd said them. I knew better than to take things out on Roberta, this wasn't her fault.

She sighed. "I went fucking *ballistic* on Rodney, *didn't I?* That was *so* embarrassing..." She shook her head a little, cringing with renewed regret. I instantly felt like shit for bringing it up.

"No crazier than *I* went," I scoffed, trying to take the misplaced heat off of her. "I mean I saw Garrett with Annette and I just...I saw *red!* I had to get out of there before I actually inflicted physical *violence*," I admitted, breathless from the traumatic memory.

"Yeah, you looked *scary*. I thought you were going to drag her out of there by the hair. Hell, I almost did *for* you! But when you took off, I knew you needed me," she admitted.

I sat in silence, ingesting everything that happened.

"It must be true love then," Roberta piped up, trying to lighten the mood. "Only true love makes you do crazy things. Stupid things."

"That's for sure," I mumbled in agreement.

* * *

We got to our complex and parked. On our way up the elevator to our apartment, we chatted briefly.

"I don't know, I guess we just need to establish some ground rules. Garrett and I... we never put a *title* on what we are. We never said we'd be monogamous or *anything*. I guess I just assumed," I shrugged.

"*Never* assume with men," Roberta said pointedly. "With men you have to tell them the clear cut rules in black and white. Leave no room for gray area, or they will assume they can get away with anything."

I nodded, then sighed. "This is getting so serious, so *fast*."

"It happens," she shrugged. "But if you really love him, you gotta be willing to work hard at *keeping* him."

I sighed again, dismayed.

"Corinne, he's just as crazy about *you,* as you are *him*. You don't need to worry," she reassured me.

The elevator dinged and we walked out into the hall and to our apartment.

We both ate, showered, got ready, and left for work. The bonus about being your own boss, is you can show up late whenever you want. And after today's ordeal, we most definitely were *late*. At work,

I couldn't help but replay the awkward events of this morning. I'd *cried* in front of Garrett, I'd *hit* him...God, I'd *slapped* him! I'd acted like an absolute *imbecile!* And the *worst* part was, now he knew how desperately jealous I was of any other females in his life. Sure, he probably should've told me he was going to meet for breakfast with his *ex-girlfriend*. But would I have been *okay* with it even then? *Hell no!* But in the same token, Garrett was innocent like that. He was friendly, unassuming, and so naturally lovable. I wasn't sure if he *had* any enemies, *male or female!* I couldn't hold it against him, that he was so naturally trusting. I still wish I had reacted with at least *half* the passion that I had. I felt more transparent than ever.

At five o'clock we closed up the shop and headed home. I got dressed casually in jeans, a soft t-shirt and sandals, then headed over to Garrett's apartment in Roberta's car. Sometimes I felt guilty about using her car for my own personal needs, but when my car had broken down in the first few months of us living together, Roberta had insisted on us sharing one. She said it was pointless for me to waste money on getting my own car when all we ever did, we did *together*. We worked together and were together all the time anyway. And I had no love life up until *now*, so it *did* make sense. I was aware that pretty soon we'd have to outgrow this arrangement of ours, especially now that we were *both* in

223

relationships. At least, I *hoped* I'd still be in one after tonight.

I parked beside Garrett's red Camaro in the lot and made my way up, via the elevator. I knocked tentatively on the door. My heart was thumping warily in my chest. He pulled open the door and forced a polite smile at me that made my insides twist in discomfort. He looked handsome as ever, in a thin t-shirt and worn jeans. His hair was ruffled and sexy. I took a moment to admire him. His features were striking. His wide, green, intelligent eyes always conveyed the emotions he tried to hide. His manly jawline was irresistible and lined with scruff. I wanted him to myself. *Was that such a crime?* Why did things have to be more complicated than that? Why did there have to be *labels?*

I walked in and he closed the door behind me, avoiding eye contact. Another bad sign.

"So, I'm here...what did you want to talk about?" I shrugged, standing awkwardly in the middle of the dining room.

Garrett silently gestured for me to take a seat on the couch. I swallowed the ever growing lump in my throat and sat. I watched him as he deposited himself beside me. He sighed and took a long look at me. "You look beautiful tonight, Corinne. You know, I've always thought you were beautiful. Ever since the first time I saw you," he said mournfully.

My cheeks warmed with surprise, but I couldn't fully appreciate his words when he looked and sounded so *sad*. He paused for a moment, then took my hands gently. "What *happened* today? Who *was* that girl? Because I didn't recognize her," he stared into my eyes.

The lump in my throat grew heavier. I shook my head. "I don't know," I answered honestly. "I've never acted like that before."

"It's my fault, I know that. I should've told you. I just...I know how you feel about Annette," he began to explain.

"Well yeah, Garrett. What did you *expect?* Me to be *happy* about it? You were *engaged* at one time!" I blurted out.

"You know that's *long* over!" He stood abruptly, withdrawing his hands.

I watched him, my mouth falling open. He sat back down slowly. "You can't be angry with me that I'm friends with my ex! I like to maintain friendships, not burn all bridges when a relationship is over! So *forgive* me, Corinne, for being a *decent* human being!"

I flinched back from his words. "*Excuse me?* What is *that* supposed to mean?"

Garrett looked away and shook his head. "*Nothing*, it means nothing."

"You know *what?* It doesn't even *matter!* You don't want to be serious with me *anyway!* If you *did*, you would've already asked me to be your *girlfriend!*" I slapped my hands back down on my lap in emphasis.

He looked appalled. "I—*girlfriend?* You're *more* to me than *that* and you *know* it! You're my *best* friend and—"

I felt sick. What was I *thinking?* It was clear now what I was to Garrett. I wasn't *wife* material. I wasn't even *girlfriend* material. He would *never* take me seriously. I was just a fuck buddy to him. I couldn't believe I didn't see it before. What an idiot I was, preserving my whole heart for him for all of these years. He didn't deserve it. All of that time and emotion had been *wasted.*

"And that's all I'm ever going to be," I breathed, barely able to speak.

Garrett paled. "No—*no*, Corinne! Don't *do* this. Don't you *dare* do this," he accused. His voice was more raw than before, his green eyes were haunted.

I stood slowly. "Don't *pretend* for *my* sake," I snapped. "You don't have to pretend anymore. I'm a big girl and I can *take* it." My eyes were glittering with unshed tears, but I didn't care.

He jumped to his feet and I held my hands out in warning.

"Pretend *what*, Corinne? That I *love* you! You *know* I love you. You *know* that!" He pleaded.

I shook my head vehemently. "I don't want your pity. Just—just let me *go*." I started backing towards his front door and he followed me cautiously. When I was a few feet from the door, his eyes looked more panicked.

"*Stop*. Corinne? Don't leave. Don't leave like this. *Stay* and *talk* to me!" He reached for me.

I moved back swiftly, knowing if I let him touch me, I would never let him stop. But he managed to grab my wrist, and pulled me to him. He planted his lips on mine, and I sobbed, withdrawing.

"*Don't*," I commanded, with fire in my eyes, pushing him back.

He let go of me and stumbled backward. The truth is, I'd never been more scared in my life. The power he had over me frightened me and all I wanted to do was run away before he had the chance to destroy me. Only *he* could do that. Only *he* could demolish me, leaving me in a pile of forgotten ashes. Because if there was *any* chance that he loved me less than I loved him, I wouldn't be able to handle it.

I took a deep breath, already feeling nauseated about what I was about to have to do. I met his eyes. "You were just a good *fuck*, Garrett. I *lied*. I *don't* love you. I just wanted to *sleep* with you," I enunciated each word, hoping my words would cut him deep enough for him to let me go.

But he stepped up to me nose to nose, his eyes fixed on mine like green fire. "*Liar*," he accused.

I backed up, frightened.

"It's *true!* I just wanted to *fuck* you. I'm only sorry that I let it get this *far*," I added, my voice cracked and his eyes flashed with pain.

He recoiled away from me, like I was a disease. "You're a coward, Corinne. If you want to leave, then just go," he said, in defeat.

His words rattled my core. I paused for a moment, willing myself to move. "I'm already gone," I whispered. Then with trembling hands, I opened the door and slipped out.

CHAPTER THIRTY-TWO
Detonator

I heard a sigh from above me. "Do I even *need* to ask?"

I lie sprawled across my hard bedroom floor, surrounded by liquor bottles. Louise laid on top of me and began to lick my face in hopes to rouse me at Roberta's entrance.

I rolled to my side. "I'm a detonator," I murmured, my voice slurred and my cheek pressed against the cool wood. "Anything I touch goes..." I held my right hand out for emphasis, making a fist then splaying my fingers out, imitating a bomb exploding. "*Kablooey*," I finished.

Roberta crouched down beside me, her long hair hung above me like a dark curtain. "That *bad*, huh?"

My eyes strained to meet hers. "I *told* him he was just a booty call."

"You really think he *believed* that?" She scoffed.

My eyes fell back to the wooden floor. Louise purred, sauntering around me. "Sure *looked* like he did. Either way...he's *pissed*. I messed up. So. Bad."

"It was *one* bad night, Corinne. *One* bad day. *One* fight. Over *years* and *years* of friendship. You really think you *ruined* your relationship?" Roberta asked skeptically, inspecting my face gently.

"Yes."

She rose and I rolled over to my back, staring up at her. "You look nice. Where are you going?" I appraised her.

She was wearing blue bell bottom pants and a tight white tank top. Her long dark hair was silken and curled at the ends. She wore nude heels.

"Thanks," she smiled briefly. "Well *work*, for starters. I'm assuming you're taking a *personal* day?" She raised a brow.

"Yes ma'am," I nodded.

"Okay and then after, I have a date with Rodney at The Olde Pink House."

A huge lump formed in my throat. "*The*—The Olde Pink House? *G—Garrett* took me there once. You're going to like it," I muttered, then reached for a random empty bottle, not even bothering to read the label. I tipped it back until the last drop landed in my throat.

Roberta reached down and took the bottle from me. "No more booze, Corinne," she scolded, then grabbed up the other remaining bottles.

I scowled at her.

"I'll allow you one day to wallow, but *tomorrow*, you're getting off your ass and coming to *work!*" She pointed at me.

I saluted her. "Yes, boss," I hiccuped.

Her face softened. "And I *love* you. And I promise *everything* is going to be *fine*...you'll see. *Any* moment now he's going to call or text you," she said with forced cheer.

I stared, not believing it for a minute. "Have fun at dinner."

"Thanks," she smiled. "By the way, I got you a little present," she smiled conspiratorially, blushing.

My eyebrows lifted in surprise. "Oh? For what?"

Roberta's lips twisted in amusement. "Oh, let's just call it a little 'pick me up' gift," she grinned mischievously.

"Okay...well, thank you. You didn't have to do that," I smiled appreciably. She was so thoughtful.

"It's no big deal. Actually...it is kind of *big*..." She giggled.

"What?"

"Nothing," she cleared the naughty expression from her face. "I left it in your top drawer," she said, matter-of-factly.

She turned on her heel, quickly walking away from me, before I could ask why. She left me lying on the floor, confused. I listened to the sound of her heels click-clacking through the house, moving further away from me by the second.

I couldn't help it. "*But if it's so big, then how did it fit in my drawer?*" I called out into the open space.

"You'll *see!*" I heard Roberta call back. "Have fun!"

Before I could ask another question, I heard the sound of the front door open and shut.

But how would I 'have fun' alone? I wondered to myself. She knew the condition I was in. What a strange thing to say...

Shaking it off, I reached for my phone, sliding the screen aside. *No messages, no missed calls. Nothing.*

God, the silence *hurt*. It had only been *one* night since I talked to Garrett, and I wasn't sure how I was going to make it.

I climbed to my feet, deciding to see what the fuss was about this 'mystery gift' I'd been left. I stumbled sloppily over to my dresser and opened the top drawer. A small white card lay atop of the gift. I picked it up and read it.

Every girl needs one. —Love, Roberta.

I scrunched my nose up in confusion, setting the card aside and eyeing the gift suspiciously.

A long object was wrapped in purple tissue paper. "Doesn't look very *big* to me," I mumbled mockingly to myself. I picked it up and it felt heavy and hard. "What the hell?" I unwrapped the tissue paper and instantly dropped the 'gift' back into the drawer. It landed with a heavy *thunk*.

It was a hot pink vibrator, a big one.

Roberta had officially given up on me. I'd been given the 'eternal spinster' gift. After the initial shock had worn off, I decided to examine the foreign object further. I toyed with the settings, frightened by the highest setting the most. I considered throwing it away, but instead replaced it back into the drawer, opting to keep it in case of emergencies. I wasn't feeling that desperate tonight.

I sighed. "I have to pull myself together," I decided.

By the time Roberta had come home, I had cleaned the apartment, showered, cooked myself dinner and even baked us cookies.

She walked in and sniffed the air suspiciously. "Do I smell...*cookies?*"

"Yes. I *baked*," I lifted my chin proudly.

Roberta set down her purse. "*Ooo* yummy," she rushed over.

She sat down at the counter and helped herself to few, scooping them onto the small plates I provided. I pushed the opened bottle of wine at her and a glass chute. "Cookies *and* wine? *Ms. Powell*, are you trying to *seduce* me?" She poured herself a glass, grinning widely.

I shrugged. "I felt bad for bailing on you at work today," I admitted.

"Aw, that's ok," she answered.

I lifted my glass and we clinked glasses together.

Roberta took a bite and closed her eyes in ecstasy. "*Mmmm...* oh my *God*, you made the ones with the cinnamon," she moaned.

I smirked. "*Yes*, I did." They were a specialty of mine and everyone I'd ever made them for always asked for more.

"Thanks for my *gift* by the way," I quipped sarcastically.

Roberta spluttered into her wine glass. "Did you like it?" She laughed shamelessly.

I pretended to be thoughtful. "Well, I *can* say that I've *never* gotten a gift quite like *that* before."

Roberta laughed even harder, choosing not to question if I'd used it. Even *she* had her limits when it came to TMI. "I thought you'd like it."

"Oh, it's one-of-a-kind, for sure," I commented.

"Actually, I have one in lime green," she snickered.

"Roberta!" I scolded. *What did I say about TMI?*

"*What?* I had to test the product out before giving it to my bestie!"

"Okay! No more about this, please!" I hid my face with my free hand. My cheeks were effectively burning bright red.

"Okay," she laughed, "and you're welcome."

We ate in silence for a few minutes until I noticed Roberta's cheeks deepen in pink.

"What is it?" I half smiled, with curiosity in my voice. *Please don't bring up vibrators again*, I worried to myself.

"*Well...*" Her eyes twinkled. "I was just thinking about how *funny* it was that you made these cookies. Almost like you *knew* there was going to be a special occasion to celebrate."

I scrunched up my face. "*What* are you talking about?"

Roberta tried to hold back her smile, but it wasn't working. She held up her right hand, and to my horror, a sparkly band glittered on her ring finger.

"Rodney asked me to *marry* him tonight!" She gleamed.

My jaw fell open and I was momentarily struck speechless. Inside, I felt the raw panic clawing its way up my throat. The coldness threatened to spread throughout me like frostbite. This couldn't have happened at a *worse* time for me. But *this* wasn't about *me. This* was about *Roberta!* And if the tables were reversed, I'd want *her* to be happy for *me.* And when I *really* thought about it, I *was* happy for her. She *deserved* happiness, she *deserved* to be loved. So, I swallowed back all of my own grief and did what *any* good friend would do. I squealed and threw my arms around her neck, hugging her and congratulating her.

"Thank you, *thank you.* I was *so* surprised. I had *no* idea he had *planned* this," she gushed.

Then I sat and listened to the story of Rodney's romantic proposal. He had put the ring into her champagne glass and had a live band play their song.

"So...I have a very important question to ask you. Actually, it's not a question. You *have* to do it. I mean, *please?*" She was smiling so big, I'd never seen her look so *happy* before. She was actually *glowing.*

"*Anything*, Roberta. You're my *best friend*," I breathed.

"We want to elope in *Vegas!* Say you'll come and be my maid of honor!" She bubbled up with joy.

"*Yes*," I said simply, shrugging my shoulders. "Just say *when*," I added.

"*Next week!*" She squealed reaching over to hug me.

My whole *body* rejected the statement. "*What?*" I whispered into her hair.

She pulled back and looked into my eyes, her own were wide and earnest. "I *know* it's *crazy*, but when you know, *you know*. I'm *not* waiting. I want to marry Rodney as *soon* as possible!"

I shook my head to clear it. "Er—yes, I mean, *yes! Whatever* you want. I mean, *you're* the *bride*...?"

Her eyes widened even more and she jumped up and down. "*I'm* the bride! I'm *the bride!*" She left my side and started to dance around the kitchen.

I giggled, in spite of myself. She was *joyous*. Her own happiness made my *unhappiness* suddenly seem insignificant.

She stopped dancing and a strange look crossed her features.

"What is it?" I asked, worried.

"There's just *one* more little thing I need to tell you," she held her fingers together, leaving a pinch of air between them.

"*What?*" I asked, already feeling my face fall.

"Garrett is coming."

CHAPTER THIRTY-THREE
Shotgun Wedding

"You're *sure* you're not pregnant?" I checked with Roberta again.

She laughed. "No *way!* Me and Rodney don't plan on procreating for a while. So, no worries there!"

We stood in the same little boutique we always frequented when Roberta needed her dresses custom made, called Bonnie's Boutique. But *this* time, it was a *wedding* dress she was being fitted for. I watched as Bonnie, the little waif of a woman with a puff of white hair, puttered around her. She carefully inserted pins into the thin, silk fabric. The fabric clung tightly to Roberta's perfectly curved hourglass frame. It was a simple gown, Roberta hadn't wanted to make a big fuss of it. It was a *Vegas* wedding after all and she'd wanted it to be as inexpensive as possible. Which literally made *no* sense to me. A girl who'd lived in the lap of luxury for many years, wanted a *simple* wedding. Maybe that fact made her even *more* awesome.

"Haha good. I'm not sure I'm ready to share my best friend *that* much. Babies are little attention stealers and I already have to lose you to *Rodney*," I blanched.

Roberta giggled, pleased. "I already *told* you, you're not *losing* me! Well, at least not for a few months anyway. While we look for our *perfect* place. And even *then,* I told you you were welcome to live *with* us!" she insisted brightly.

The sad part is, I knew she *meant* it. But the thought made me sick. *All of it.* Losing Roberta, becoming a third wheel at their happy home, or becoming a spinster in my own lonely one.

"I think that looks good, what do you think?" Bonnie politely ignored our conversation, as she and Roberta inspected the dress' adjustments in the body length mirror in front of us.

"I do too," Roberta nodded after a critical-eyed inspection. "Your turn Corinne," she said pointedly, stepping aside and gently moving me by the hips in front of the mirror.

I stared at my reflection, my fuchsia colored dress was strapless and looked pretty against my skin. I gazed unseeingly at myself in the mirror's reflection as Bonnie tugged and poked at me. "Oh well, I'll always have *Louise*," I lamented. "A woman and her *cat*," I bit out the words.

"Roberta snickered behind me. "Are you forgetting that we *work* together? We'll see each other *every day!*" She reminded me.

Her head poked above mine in the reflection. She was smiling adorably, and I couldn't help but cheer up when she did that.

I sighed. "I *know*. I'm being a big baby about this," I admitted.

Roberta came around to my side. "That looks good, Bonnie," she nodded.

Bonnie nodded back. "Let me just write down the measurements and I'll be right back with you to help you pick out shoes," she excused herself.

As soon as she left, Roberta moved to my side. "He still hasn't called?" She asked, her eyes sympathetically sliding to the floor.

"No, and he's not *going* to, and I don't *expect* him to. He's probably going to get back together with Annette. She's more his type anyway. They make sense, like peanut butter and jelly. He doesn't want someone like me," I pouted, my hands on my hips.

Roberta lifted my chin, forcing me to meet her eyes. A wide grin spread across her face. "Oh please, peanut butter and jelly is *boring* anyway! They're *too* well matched and that's why they didn't last. My bet is *he's* just as miserable as *you*." I scoffed. "A little bird told me he looked like hell at his tux fitting today. Like he hadn't slept a *wink*," she encouraged with a sly smirk.

I fought the urge to look pleased. "You *mean* he was up all night with some young thing again?" I quipped, raising my eyebrows.

She shook her head slowly, widening her crystal blue eyes at me in emphasis. "I *mean* he was up all night dreaming of some young thing that he had a taste of, and now he can't get her *off* of his mind!" She laughed haughtily and I turned red.

"Whatever, Roberta," I smiled.

Bonnie came back with the measurements and we resumed our appointment. But the whole time I couldn't help but let my thoughts wander to Roberta's words. Was that *true?* Had he been missing *me* as bad as *I* was missing *him?* I *hoped* it was. Because if it *was*, it meant we still had a chance.

* * *

One evening when Roberta was out with Rodney, I decided to call my mom. She answered on the third ring. "*Corinne?*"

"Hey, mom."

"*Hi honey!* To what do I owe this honor?" She teased.

I laughed awkwardly. I knew I was guilty of not calling her enough. "I just thought I should let you know that I'll be flying out to Vegas next week. Roberta's getting married," I worked to sound enthusiastic about that last part, but I wasn't sure I was convincing.

She tried to sound surprised at first, but then eventually admitted to me, "I know. Her parents told me. They weren't the most *pleased* about the whole *Vegas* elopement thing, but they're happy for her nonetheless! How are *you* feeling about it?" Her voice turned sympathetic at the end, and I shrank down inside myself.

"*Fine*, mom. I mean, I'm *happy* for her. She's my *best* friend." That last part sounded really sad, and I mentally kicked myself for it.

"Oh *honey*, I know it's *a lot*. You know you're *always* welcome to come back home and live for a while?" She offered.

I laughed sadly. "*Thanks* mom, but I'd really just like some help choosing a new place."

"Oh *sure!* I'd *love* to help! Just let me know when you're ready!" She enthused.

I sighed in relief. "That'd be great, mom. So how's dad?" I inquired.

Her voice warmed with fondness, as it always did when we spoke of my father. "Oh, you know your father, always up to something. His latest craze is online shopping. I think he's *addicted,*" she whispered conspiratorially into the phone.

I stifled a laugh. "That sounds interesting."

"Oh, *it is*," she giggled.

"You know who I saw yesterday?" She changed the subject suddenly. Something about the lift in her voice warned me.

"...*Who?*" I asked with caution.

"*Garrett Simmons!* At the post office! My *goodness!* The *man* he's grown into! *Corinne*, you should *see* him now! Have you seen him *lately?*"

245

I could just imagine the way she'd be holding her hand over her heart in a gesture that suggested he almost gave her a heart attack.

My whole body flushed in pleasure at my recollection of just how *much* I'd *seen* of the man himself. "Yes, mom, I have. We...we, um...recently had dinner." *That sounded innocent enough, right?*

"*Oh!* You *have?* Oh, honey, are you *dating?*" I heard the shock of pleasure in her voice.

"*No*—no, mom. We just... caught up," I tried to save myself. *We caught up a lot,* I thought to myself, perversely.

"Oh...well he acted like he wanted to *see* you again. *Very much,*" she informed me, hopeful. "You should give him a call," she suggested.

I rolled my eyes. "Sure thing, mom."

"*Corinne,*" she scolded.

"*What?*" I asked, annoyed.

"You know that boy's been absolutely *in love* with you since the third grade. Give him a *chance,*" she pleaded.

"*What* are you talking about mom?" I asked, in shock.

"*How* have you not *known* this, honey? *Tell me* you've *known?* It's been *clear* as *day*," she reprimanded me.

I felt too exposed, and the fact that my *mom* could plainly see what *I'd* mistaken for years, filled me with shame. "I have to go mom," I urged.

"Okay honey. But *remember* what I said, and call me when you're ready to go house hunt! And call me when you leave to, *and* land in Vegas. And don't forget to take plenty of *pictures!*" She rushed.

"I *will* mom, I *will*," I tried to dial down the exasperation in my voice. "Tell dad I love him for me, will you?"

"Of course, dear. And Corinne?"

"Yes, mom?"

"*Call Garrett*."

CHAPTER THIRTY-FOUR

Vegas, Baby!

No missed calls. No missed messages. No missed e-mails. All inboxes "Garrett-less". It'd been three weeks since we last spoke to or saw each other. The man knew how to stay silent. The foreboding thought in the back of my mind remained, that he hated me. In fact, it played like a mantra in my mind. It served as a reminder, every time I picked up my phone and found he still hadn't contacted me.

He hates you. He hates you. He hates you.

But despite my mom's sound advice, and my own sense of guilt and remorse, I couldn't bring myself to contact him and apologize. I was too afraid that he'd actually say the words out loud. *"I hate you, Corinne."*

As I packed my bag for Vegas, the butterflies in my stomach seemed to grow to the size of hummingbirds. An hour later, I sat at the windowsill of our apartment, looking out into the street below.

"Ready?" I heard Roberta ask.

I turned and saw her beaming. I jumped up immediately, wiping the mopey look off of my face. "Of course!" I grabbed my bag.

We Uber-ed to the airport and boarded our plane soon after. Roberta had two other of her model friends come to be the bridesmaids, their names were Sheila and Margaret. I think they mostly just wanted to come to party. *But who could blame them?* It *was* Vegas. On the airplane, I kept looking for Garrett's tall body to enter.

Roberta caught my eye. "He's not on this flight," she informed me.

Chagrined, I turned to face the front and stuck in my ear buds. We had to stop once in Denver, but the plane change was almost immediate. We barely had time to grab a snack and board. I'd chosen a glossy gossip magazine to flip through to keep me entertained for the remainder of the flight. We arrived in Las Vegas at the perfect time...dusk. The city lights were just starting to sparkle. The girls began chattering excitedly and I too, set down the magazine and became alert.

I was embarrassed that my mind had been so occupied with thoughts of Garrett, that I had completely forgotten to ask before, "which hotel is ours, Roberta?" I peered out the window at the buildings below.

She had booked it online and never informed me of its name, and *I* had never asked. "Cesar's Palace," she pointed below in its direction with her chin.

"Ohh..." I said, looking down. "It's *nice*," my eyebrows flew up in appreciation.

"That's where they filmed *The Hangover*," Margaret piped up, clearly filled with glee with the idea of *us* staying there.

There was a murmured acknowledgement from our group before we all had to sit back and prepare to land. It had been a four hour trip and my nerves were frazzled, leaving me feeling wiry. My stomach was in knots over the inevitable idea of seeing Garrett. I almost wished he *had* been on the same plane, so I could've got it over with already.

After we landed and retrieved our bags, we took a shuttle to our hotel. The plan was to have Roberta's bachelorette party tonight, followed by her and Rodney's elopement at the Little White Wedding Chapel tomorrow night. Roberta had already booked our tickets to see the "Thunder From Down Under" tonight and it was all anyone could talk about on the ride to the hotel.

"I heard if you pay a little extra, they'll meet you backstage for a *private* dance," Sheila scandalized.

"You're *disgusting!*" Margaret shook her head.

When we arrived at our hotel, my nerves finally started to subside. I started worrying less about seeing Garrett, and began to see this for what it *really* was. A trip for *Roberta*. A trip with *friends*. *Girl* friends, that is.

Our suite was polished and spacious. Mine and Roberta's room adjoined with Margaret and Sheila's. Not that it mattered anyway, Roberta was already getting dressed for the evening's events before I knew it. I tried to hide my disappointment when I found out that we were leaving so soon. I had just gotten used to the plush feel of the hotel bed, and my sore muscles had just felt an increment of relief, before I knew I couldn't get comfortable.

We got dressed in our cutest outfits. Dresses, skirts and heels galore. I flat-ironed my hair until it was sleek and smooth. I wore a white dress that flattered my skin tone, with fire red heels and lipstick. Roberta wore a baby pink beaded gown with matching heels that was just the right amount of fun for the evening. When Margaret and Sheila sauntered into our room, the excitement was palpable.

"*Yes!* We look so *hootttt!*" Roberta gathered everyone for a group picture before heading out the door.

We made our way down the halls and elevators, and through the lobby.

"*We're in Vegas, baby!*" Roberta shouted as we exited our hotel.

A white limo pulled up in the drive of Cesar's palace and I turned to Roberta questionably. She nodded with a sparkle in her eye. "*Yes*, that is for *us! Rodney* ordered it." She danced a goofy little jig.

My mouth fell open in delight and we all headed over to it, climbing in. There were bottles of champagne waiting inside. We popped open a few and helped ourselves. We were having so much fun, I almost didn't ask, but part of me had to know.

"Hey Roberta, where are the boys tonight?"

Her eyes flashed briefly with concern, before she answered. "Rodney and the boys are going to hit up some strip clubs tonight, and then after we're all done, we're going to meet up and all party together."

I felt those words sink in. '*Meet up and party together*' in particular flashed in my mind like a Vegas casino sign.

Roberta noticed the look on my face, before I lifted my glass and took a long, deep gulp.

"*Corinne*," she coaxed. My eyes slid to hers. "It's going to be *fine*. It's going to be *fun*, you'll *see! Don't worry!*" She tried to ease my anxiety.

I gathered my emotions, tying them back like I would my hair when I pull it into a tight ponytail. There would be time to deal with them *later*. She didn't need to be fussing over *me* on *her* wedding-moon.

"Oh, I *know!*" I did my best 'party girl' voice impression.

Then to prove that I wasn't going to be a "Debbie downer", I stood and pressed the button to open the window on the roof of the limo. I stuck my head out and screamed, "*hey, Las Vegas!* My best friend is getting *married* tomorrow!"

CHAPTER THIRTY-FIVE
One Drunk Night

After the limo ride and the pulse pounding, hormone inducing, meaty man show (in which Roberta almost forgot she was engaged and tried to take home 'Umberto, the Italian Stallion'), was over with, we did indeed meet up with the boys.

The girls were still fired up over the show, adrenaline was running high and we were carrying those gigantic plastic, neon margaritas around. The 'Thunder' boys had gifted us with plastic beads and we stumbled into the bar, looking for Rodney and Garrett.

I walked behind everyone, knowing full well that my buzz alone and the high of the night wouldn't be enough to patch up my problems so easily. Roberta had already ran into Rodney's arms and the two of them were engaged in a full make-out session. Margaret and Sheila had already linked up with Rodney's two model friends Jonah and Caleb, leaving Garrett and I alone at the bar. At first, we tried to ignore each other, but eventually the gentleman in Garrett couldn't resist. He scooted on over, his big hands sliding across the wooden bar counter. He was wearing a tight smile. Although he was clearly wary and cautious, I could see the resolve in his eyes, I could *feel* it radiating out of him.

"I guess they really *are* always like that," he whispered from the corner of his mouth, giving me a sidelong glance.

And despite myself, and despite the flurry of emotions running wild through me at the sight of him, and the sound of his voice, I snickered. We hadn't spoken in weeks, but it felt like yesterday again. He had that way of just making you feel comfortable, familiar. *That* was always dangerous. He was wearing a tight black t-shirt and dark jeans. His hair was freshly cut and he smelled amazing as usual. I recklessly let the scent of him linger in my brain for a while, until memories flashed through my mind that made me blush. I looked away when our eyes met. Surely he couldn't *tell* what I'd been thinking?

He sure didn't *look* like he'd been through the ringer, like Roberta had *claimed* he had. If he *had,* he covered it up well.

"So how do *you* feel about all of this?" He gestured with his beer in hand, making an invisible circle around our little party. "The *wedding*, I mean. It's pretty *sudden*, don't you think?"

My eyebrows shot up and I answered honestly. "They've been through enough, I think. They've known each other long enough," I resolved. "Their history and all the things they have in common make me think it'll last. That and the fact that they're head over heels *in love*. I've *never* seen Roberta act that with *anyone* else," I laughed haughtily. Garrett chuckled in agreement.

I sobered, looking over at Roberta and Rodney. "I think he's the one for her," I nodded confidently, turning back to Garrett. "When you know, you know," I shrugged, repeating Roberta's words. I accidentally met Garrett's eyes when I said it, and I instantly regretted it. I looked down again and pretended to be immensely occupied with the wood work of the bar, and the beer in my hand.

"Yes, I suppose so," I heard him say beside me. His voice had gone low and strained. "Though *we've* known each other *a lot* longer," he chuckled.

I nodded, still afraid to meet his eyes again.

"You look lovely as usual," he observed aloud.

"Thank you," I muttered.

I took a deep breath and decided it was time to be the bigger person. "Garrett, I am *sorry* about what I said to you," I stared into his eyes. "You *know* it's not true. You know I'd *never* see you that way, as only..." I struggled. "A good...*fuck*," I whispered.

His eyes grew impossibly wide, and the friendly mask he wore began to slip away and show emotion. I don't think he *expected* me to apologize, or even bring up our fight. I think he expected me to do what I usually did, what I was good at, hiding and running away. My candidness had briefly shocked him into silence, before he uttered out, "of course, I know you wouldn't."

He seemed shaken up, so I drank my beer and let him absorb the information. But we didn't have long to do that, before shots were being pushed down our way, spilling all over the bar. Everyone was celebrating Roberta and Rodney's upcoming marriage and I felt guilty for getting caught in our own little tense bubble for even a moment. I swallowed down the feeling and tried to engage in the merriment before me. Garrett too, put his mask back on. I felt like something had healed between us, and that allowed me to become a fun member of the party again. I'd spoken my peace, now all that was left to do was wait. If worse came to worse, he'd at least still want me as a *friend*, still respect me, as a *person*.

* * *

We carried on after that, the night becoming more fuzzy as time went on. At some point I'd lost count of the drinks I had, the places I'd danced and the bars we'd visited. But Garrett held onto my hand the whole evening, not letting me get lost in the wild Vegas ruckus. I remember dancing with him. Even more importantly, I remember *kissing* him. Some part in the back of my brain wanted to scream out in joy at the acknowledgment. But with my mind so clouded with the haze of inebriation, I couldn't fully celebrate it. After that, everything else was a black hole. I don't remember going back to the hotel. I don't remember the limo ride. I was sure at least, I had survived *mostly* unscathed.

When I awoke, my whole body ached, and my head thrummed like a drum beat. I groaned in pain and rolled over, landing on a body. It was hard and warm and felt...*male?* Oh, shit. Oh, no. *Please don't be male!* Roberta works out a lot, *right?* But why would *she* be in *my* bed? She had her own. *Maybe she got lonely?* Maybe one of us threw up and was doctoring the other? That sounded feasible.

"Mmmrrmm," A deep voice protested. There was a shift of movement beside me in the bed.

Nope, that most definitely was *not* Roberta. That was...

I sat up, instantly alarmed and the blood rushed to my head. *Men!* This whole room *reeked* of *men!* I blinked back at my now dry contact lenses that were stuck to my eyes, until my vision cleared. Across from me, on a separate bed, was Rodney. His dark body was sprawled out over the bedsheets. *Oh my God*, I was in *their* room! My head snapped over to see the deep blue light of dawn peeking through the thick white hotel curtains. I'd spent the *night* with *Garrett* in *their* room! Something on the floor caught my attention, it was my red heel. But it was *broken*. I tilted my head at it questionably. *Where was the other?* I looked down and breathed in relief that I was at least still wearing my dress. I inspected it, overjoyed that it wasn't covered in vomit stains. My head ached and I lifted my hands to hold it, that's when I felt something *very* foreign under my fingers. It was scratchy and *lace?* I slipped it off and held it in my hands in confusion. *A veil?* Then I noticed the most stunning revelation of all. *A ring.* There was a *ring* on my *finger!* The *left* finger! It looked cheap, perhaps cubic zirconia.

"What the *fuck?*" I muttered, my voice crackling with sleep.

Garrett stirred beside me and I flinched. He reached for me in his sleep, his hand grabbing at air. But then I saw it. *His* left hand, there was a ring on it. A simple gold band, that looked like it was cheap enough to find in a Cracker Jack box. He pulled down the blankets and I could see his sleepy face. He looked absolutely wrecked.

"*Corinne?*" He furrowed his brows in confusion.

Oh no. He was just as dumbstruck as I was.

"What are you *doing* here? Is that a *wedding* veil?" He giggled nervously.

My mouth hung open, and I swallowed dryly, willing myself to speak. My phone rang, breaking the silence.

Garrett and I both stared, before I slowly slid my hand over the blankets to retrieve it.

"Hel-*hello?*" I asked in a tiny voice.

"*Corinne!* Oh my *God!* We were so *worried!* We've been looking *everywhere* for you! We thought we'd *lost* you, and then I saw the pictures from last night. Holy *shit*, Corinne! You *wild woman!* I can't *believe* you did it!" She breathed.

"*Pictures?*" Was all I could ask. "*What* pictures?"

Garrett's eyes widened, as he reached for his own phone, sliding over the screen and opening up the pictures no doubt.

"They're fucking *hilarious,* Corinne! I can't *believe* you beat me to it! You *drama queen!* Now we'll have *double* the reason to party tonight!" She squealed.

The dread that filled me was stifling, suffocating. Garrett passed over his phone, his face going ghost white. I saw myself there in the picture, wearing the same dress as I was currently still sporting, with an added veil and one red heel. Garrett held me in his arms, a cheap black bow tie was stuck to his throat. We were both smiling like fools. Scattered around us, was a very inebriated wedding party, including Roberta and Rodney. She was riding on his back, piggy back style. The words on the banner behind us, was the part where everything connected, snapping together in my brain. 'The Little White Wedding Chapel' banner hung behind us in the photo.

"You got *married!!!*" Roberta sang in delight, no doubt still drunk from the night before.

"Holy shit. *Fuck! Mother-fucking shit stick!*"

* * *

Six months later...

I sat with my feet propped up on the dusty shelf, my navy blue Converse seemed to fit right in with my old childhood memories of this place. Bright sunlight filtered in through the cracks of the ceiling. I turned over the smooth shell in my palm over and over again, remembering the way I'd felt back when Garrett had first sent them. I was different girl then, and everything was unsure. Various bags of shells were littered all over the counter, each lined with thick layers of dust, along with a few old soda RC Cola cans. A stack of old Teen Beat magazines were arranged in a short stack in the corner, held in by an old wooden crate. Various pictures of me, Roberta and Garrett, in different stages of our life, were tied together by fishing wire and hung from the ceiling. We'd had so many memories here, so many good times. A voice interrupted my reminiscing.

"Corinne? Corinne?" He called.

I reached down to pet Henry's head. His soft, curly fur tangled in my fingers. "Shh...boy," I warned him. His tail thumped on the beat-up wooden floor of the clubhouse. He whined quietly beside me.

I waited. A few minutes later, footsteps approached outside. The doorknob turned and Garrett's large figure filled the small doorway. He ducked down and squeezed into the tiny clubhouse. His eyes lit up like the sun itself when he saw me. "Thought I'd find you here. *And* you stole my dog," he accused.

"I don't know if you'd call it *stealing*, he came to me willingly," I shrugged. "I can't seem to get rid of him," I smirked, my eyes teasing.

"Is that *so?*" Garrett grinned, catching on and playing along.

I bit my lip, nodding. "It's the least I can do since Louise basically traded me in for you."

He chuckled. "It's not my fault your cat likes me so much."

Garrett looked around the clubhouse, giving it a fond once-over. "Well, are you going to stay in here *all day*, or are you going to come out and help me unpack?" He asked, absentmindedly.

I groaned.

"We can have a drink after? To celebrate our new home?"

I paused.

"Now there's a smile," he encouraged. He turned and called over his shoulder, as his bulky frame exited the door. "I also have something *else* I'd like to show you, but I don't know, you probably wouldn't be interested." He left the bait hanging.

I waited a few minutes in silence. Henry looked at me questionably. I sat up, throwing my feet off of the dusty counter and replacing the shell with its place amongst the others.

"Come on, Henry."

I pushed open the lightweight clubhouse door with Henry on my tail. It shut quietly behind me. Leaves and twigs crunched under my shoes as we made our way through the trees and up the hill, following Garrett's path. The trees finally cleared and I could see our new home on top of a green hill. I followed it up and Henry left my side, running to find Garrett. Garrett was carrying a box away from the moving truck. Henry nearly knocked him over and he laughed. Louise was there too, and she weaved herself around Garrett's ankles adoringly. He smiled down at her, before he saw me approach, setting down the box he was holding. I walked up to him with a warm smile of my own.

"Glad of you to finally join me, Mrs. Simmons," his eyes twinkled. Then he reached down into the opened box and pulled a bottle of Tequila from it.

My jaw dropped. "Interesting choice," I nodded. "I thought we were drinking *after* we unpacked?" I narrowed my eyes, smiling.

Garrett smiled conspiratorially. "This'll make things more interesting," he winked.

The End.

Made in the USA
Lexington, KY
30 November 2019

57832463R20149